To Shed A Light

Peter Aspinall

Copyright © Peter Aspinall 1998

Reprinted 2001

All rights reserved.

No part of this book may be reproduced by any means nor transmitted. Nor translated into machine language, without the written permission of the publisher.

NFS Publications
The Old Church
Flitwick Road
Ampthill
Bedfordshire
MH45 2NT

A CIP Catalogue record for this book is available from the British Library.

Printed and bound in Great Britain

ISBN 0 9532479 0 2

Acknowledgements

This book is for Denise, Luke and Jane for without their patience and understanding it would never have been completed. I would also like to thank them, and the rest of my family for allowing me to use their real names alongside all the fictitious characters.

Thanks to the very real characters in the book, portrayed fictitiously, for all their support.

Special thanks to Christine for allowing me to use her story and for all the hard work she has done in helping me to edit it.

Author's Introduction

Death is a sensitive subject that is shrouded in mystery and there is a reluctance to talk about it, even with those we love. Approaching a funeral director for advice and reassurance before the initial shock has been overcome, puts us in a very vulnerable position and yet we rarely think about contacting him before we need his services, for any sort of guidance. We cannot express ourselves clearly because we are not familiar with the procedure and we are too upset and frightened to seek help from those who can give it and yet their help in organising the funeral is so important in the grieving process.

There have been many changes over the last decade in the way funerals are organised and executed and yet we are no more comfortable about approaching the subject than we have ever been.

There can be no textbook to describe the right or wrong way to make funeral arrangements, for we will all handle it in our own way. Neither do we like to be guided by someone wearing blinkers, who can only see one approach, and sometimes, knowing what the majority of people would do in similar circumstances is just a hindrance when searching for a unique way of saying "goodbye" to someone who has been special to us. Death is the only certainty in life and therefore the details regarding our funeral should be planned whilst we are able to do so. The purpose of this book is to illustrate the importance of thinking about our own wishes, incorporating the thoughts of those we care about, without feeling that in doing so we hasten our demise.

This story describes my own death and how my family came to terms with life afterwards. It describes my feelings, my funeral and my vision for the future and illustrates the influence that we have on the people around us. I hope that by the time you get to the final chapter, you will feel that I have been able to "shed a light" on the subject.

Chapter One

It was bitterly cold and wet in the early hours of that January morning, and as I walked into the ambulance I remember looking at the blue flashing light and despite the apparent urgency found comfort from the security it seemed to offer. I lay down and pulled the red blanket around me, staring in disbelief at the roof of the vehicle. I suppose I had known all along that this would be the outcome, but I had not anticipated the relief. "Acute Appendicitis!" All these months of suffering without any clue as to what was wrong, and now at last the answer. There was no need for the siren for at three 'o clock in the morning there was no-one in the way but I would have been happier to hear it, telling the world that they had found the answer and were rushing for the cure. The journey to the hospital seemed much further than I knew it to be and when we arrived, it seemed like hours before anyone examined me and then his tests were no different to the ones I had had before. The pain returned and my temperature rose and still I lay in the cubicle waiting for another doctor to arrive. Eventually he came. The same questions, the same tests and still the pain! The x-rays did not help either. They only showed a healthy appendix and left me feeling bewildered again. For one moment, I thought they were going to send me home again because they had obviously decided that it was not appendicitis. My high temperature clinched it and they found me a bed for the night. "Observation", they called it. It was a week later before the tests and barium enema revealed the cause of the pain. "Bowel Cancer", I responded incredulously when the doctor explained that he would have to operate quickly. He said that he did not know for certain whether or not the growth was malignant, but said he thought from the size and shape, that it was. It was five-thirty on Friday evening and I had to wait until Monday morning for the operation. He said that he could cut away the 'nasty part' and then rejoin my intestine. Taking away a part of the mesentery too, would ensure that no cells had escaped to any other part of my body.

To Shed A Light

I was absolutely devastated, and I still had to tell my wife. How could I tell her without it sounding like a death sentence? Like me, she is a funeral director and certainly would not be fooled easily or fobbed off with a vague explanation. She would want to know as much as I did, probably more. I asked the ward sister if I could use her office when Denise arrived for visiting hours. She was bound to be upset and I wanted privacy. The Sister agreed and I lay back to wait for visiting time. Rehearsing the words to use was useless. Not only did I change them every time I repeated them, but I was also beginning to realise what the doctor had said, what it meant and that I was facing something that I had not experienced before. Am I really going to die?

I thought of all the words of comfort and consolation I have given to others that have been bereaved in the past, and realised for the first time how artificial it must have sounded. I was to be forty years old a few months later and although I had purchased a grave in our village cemetery to ensure that my place of burial was guaranteed, I was certainly not ready to use it yet! Suddenly, I felt scared. I thought of all the things I still wanted to do, the tasks that I had left unfinished. What about the children, my father, brothers, sister? I wondered if it would hurt, if there was a life after death, whether I would meet my mother. She had died when I was seventeen years old and I had never considered the idea of not seeing her again, until that moment. I looked around and saw the nurses going about their duties as normal. No hint that I had cancer! No recognition that there was anything different happening now. Routine temperature and blood pressure testing continued without any word mentioned of my new condition. The drip in my arm was getting sore and as I looked down towards it I noticed the wrist-band. Normally, I only notice them on the wrists of the deceased persons that have been collected from the mortuary. This name tag now took on a different meaning. I looked around at the other patients in the ward. Most were asleep, and those that were not simply grunted or moaned. One smiled unknowingly at me and I wondered whether or not he too was suffering the anguish and torment I felt at that time. Five minutes later, Denise arrived and it was just as bad as I thought it would be. We went into the sister's office and fell into each other's arms. A nurse came in, looked, apologised and went out again. I cannot remember how long we were in there, I only know that when we left the office for me to go back to bed, we were determined to fight this every step of the way and were determined to be positive. We cheered up and found from somewhere a new strength and determination to survive. I had some other visitors too but we were too tired and upset to appreciate their kindness. I was so glad when visiting time came to an end. As I watched the last of the visitors go, I lay back exhausted and waited for 'lights out', so that I could weep in private without anyone knowing. I slept very little that night and just lay analysing everything and asking over and over again, the inevitable question, "Why me?" I determined to make amends for any wrongdoing in my life and planned all the good I would do, if only I am given an opportunity. It almost sounded like a condition. No one could let me die when there was so much more to be done. Then without warning, a buzzer sounded and trolleys were being rushed about, voices raised and then my curtains were closed quickly around my bed. When it dawned on me that my neighbour was in trouble, my own vulnerability was again emphasised. It must have been about twenty minutes later when all was quiet again. My curtains were opened and I lay there looking at an empty bed with starched sheets waiting for the next patient. It had seemed like only an hour beforehand when he had smiled at me. Perhaps he knew?

As dawn broke, I looked around the ward and then through the window to the shopping parade a short distance away. I had been shopping there myself a few weeks earlier oblivious to what happens in the ward where I lay. It was quite strange, wondering whether I would ever shop again and it all seemed so unimportant. People rushing about, pushing their way forward to be first in the queue, anxious to reach the bargains before they had been sold. The January sales had never held an attraction for me but looking out then on all the shoppers, even less so. Sunday came and went without very much happening really. Visitors came, armed with magazines, joke books and 'get well' cards, Denise staying for most of the day. We had very little opportunity to discuss very much with the constant flow of well-wishers throughout the day, which was a source of comfort in many ways and frustrating in others. Eventually, the last visitor left and I was alone with Denise who had stayed to chat for a while before going home. Her strength and support was vital if I was to survive and her encouragement was unfailing. Only when I telephoned her early next morning only to find her already in tears, did I wonder whether her confidence and optimism was purely for my benefit, but she assured me that it was only a momentary lapse and that in the main she had been fine. Consoled with this thought, I slept awhile but it was a fitful sleep full of tension and restlessness. By evening I was wide awake with no hope it seemed of sleeping again, until forced to under the anaesthetic next morning. It was about midnight when all was quiet when one of the junior nurses crept over to my bed and sat beside me.' 'Are you alright?'' she said. She looked and sounded as if she had all the answers. Her pleasant approach, her tenderness and obvious care was touching and even when I answered in the affirmative she knew that it was far from being true. She spent ten minutes explaining that she knew that many of my days were spent caring for those who had died from cancer and she understood that I had frequently seen on death certificates the words, "carcinoma of the colon" as the cause of death and realised how difficult it was for me to divorce myself from these forms at this time. She reminded me though, that I only see those that are unfortunate enough to die and that a far greater percentage of patients get better and live much improved lives. She was lucky! Her statistics were better than mine. She filled me with a new sense of purpose and Denise was delighted when I passed this information on to her the next morning. Her own research confirmed this for she had not been idle either. She had read as much about it as she could and reckoned to be quite an expert on the region. My only grey area now was the thought that it may have already spread to other areas, not so easily treated and I had to wait until after the operation, indeed until after their tests had been carried out, before I could be certain.

I had so many different clergy visit me that people in the ward were beginning to think that I was a hopeless case, with death imminent, or a religious maniac. They were all friends and colleagues who I had met professionally, and whose comfort, sense of humour and genuine concern were great sources of comfort to me. Borin, affectionately known as 'Brin', was my greatest source of strength amongst those clergy and a daily visitor, a fantastic support to Denise during that time and a true friend. I could not believe the number of 'get well' cards I was receiving and was convinced that Denise had been telephoning everyone and persuading them that it would spur me on if I was to receive confirmation in the form of a card that there was something to get better for. I had promised to telephone Denise as soon as I could after the operation, to let her know that I was recovering. I was thinking about this when the male nurse came round to shave me in readiness for the operation and that soon brought me back to reality. How embarrassing! Looking around and thinking of England whilst all this was going on, I noticed the "nil by mouth" sign above my headboard and could not help thinking that this was only slightly worse than having only water. How I longed for a proper meal again. Twelve stones in weight may have been unsightly, but it was a more desirable image than the nine stones I had reduced to. Only my pyjamas fitted me, and only because they had been purchased for the occasion. I could tell that this change in appearance was upsetting for my family and my father had certainly been devastated by my sudden deterioration. For him, the word cancer was merely a reminder of the experience he had nursing my mother during her illness, and the thought that she had not survived was not helping him much either. It saddened me to watch him leave the hospital in tears, convinced that this was the beginning of the end. I tried to reassure him, but I am not convinced it worked. The nurse came round to give me my 'pre-med' and before long I was on my way to theatre.

When I came round, I was back on the ward feeling a bit the worse for wear, but almost intact. The anaesthetic wore off quickly and I was able to telephone Denise much earlier than she had anticipated and I remember how thrilled she was to hear my voice, which gave my morale a boost too. I dozed again and when I next awoke I was conscious of the catheter that had been put in during the operation. It did not take long to pull that out, although I regretted it as soon as I had done so. Fortunately, as I had been so determined not to have it, they decided not to replace it and I felt like the naughty boy that had his own way. I was not so fortunate with the naso-gastric tube. I had dreaded the thought of having to swallow that down at some point after the operation and had asked for this to be put in place during the operation. This they had achieved, but I remember the staff nurse coming round to adjust it, as she did not think it was doing the job properly. "This is too small for this job," she exclaimed, and promptly took it out and fetched another for me to swallow down. I thanked her very much for her help! The next day the physiotherapists came round, and I must admit that I had not expected or welcomed their visit. When it hurts like mad to cough, why do they insist that you do it? It was a feeble effort on my part and they were clearly not impressed because they visited me on a regular basis. Laughing, as I found out to my cost, was even worse than coughing and I had to make it clear to Denise when she visited that jokes, funny stories or anything that was likely to make me laugh was definitely out! My request lasted about five minutes and because I had mentioned it, it was impossible to look at each other without starting to laugh. At one point, we could restrain ourselves no longer and laughed helplessly for several minutes. When I eventually reached the point where I no longer knew whether to laugh or cry, we controlled each other. From that moment on, I had no pain when I coughed or laughed and my next demonstration satisfied the physiotherapists and I had seen the last of them. It seemed like months since I had eaten anything and I was desperate for something. I was surprised how my taste buds had changed in the meantime and everything was different. I started to drink and then eventually was able to have something solid. Going to the toilet for the first time was a long while happening, but it was a condition to be satisfied before I could be discharged. I thought that was a hurdle, until I tried to walk to the end of the ward. Trailing my mobile drip carrier behind me, and often using it as a support, I gradually made it there and back and knew that my stay in hospital was nearing an end. Suddenly, I felt vulnerable again. Whilst I

To Shed A Light

was desperate to get home, I was scared to leave the security of the hospital, and grateful too to the nurses and the doctors who had looked after me. I was quite looking forward to my convalescence at home and Denise had recorded lots of films for me to watch. I had lots to read and a whole list of things to achieve, but in the event, the time flew and despite the shock of trying to build up my strength again, which was much more difficult than I had anticipated, I was able to return to work earlier than expected and surprised everyone with the progress I had made. I remember taking Jodie, our golden retriever, for a walk for the first time and delighted with the smell of the mud along the lane. Being alive was tremendous and no longer taken for granted. I wondered how long that feeling would last.

I would love to be able to report now on the progress I made and the new-found opportunities to live my life to the full, sharing every moment with my family. It is true to say that the x-rays were clear and that the cancer had all been removed and in theory, here began the makings of a wonderful end to the story. The whole experience of being very ill and those desperate feelings of loss and sadness at the prospect of dying had left their mark. Without doubt, life would never be quite the same again. I had a new outlook on life and a determination to survive and a desire to make the most of the lessons I had learned. How fragile and precious life is and how important it is to live each day as if it were the last! I had a few more years of living, some of which is important enough to reflect on later, but about six years ago, some five years after I had been discharged from hospital, I decided to return to the ward with some chocolates for the nurses. It had not been the first time I had been back, in fact I had been a regular visitor over the period and I am sure that the nurses looked forward to my visits almost as much as I did, but because some of them had been on the night shift when I visited the last time, I decided to go back to see them too. I took the lift to the second floor where the St. Agnes ward was, and to my horror, the room was empty. Not a soul nor stick of furniture was in sight and I wandered back down the stairs to the floor below to see if I had got off the lift too soon, but everything was normal on that floor. I stopped one of the nurses and

11

To Shed A Light

asked for directions to the St. Agnes ward but she just replied, "Oh! that ward's closed now. Cut backs I have been told." I gave her the chocolates I had been carrying and made for the exit. I do not remember much after this. I know I walked out of the hospital feeling absolutely wretched and was heading towards the car. I remember vaguely seeing a flashing blue light and hearing a siren but I did not see the vehicle which hit me. I lay unconscious in the road until help arrived and I was taken back into the accident and emergency unit of the hospital. Denise was planning our supper when the policeman arrived. By the time she arrived at the hospital, it was too late. I never regained consciousness.

Chapter Two

To be told that someone you love may be dying from cancer and having to clutch at anything that may revive the hope for better news, is bad enough, but having fought the fight and seemingly won, with tremendous plans to live every day in future with renewed vitality, only to have them all totally dashed by this unbelievable news, is beyond our comprehension.

"Numbed" is the only word I can think of to describe the way that Denise felt when told of my death, and although she recognised the words that were being said, too much of her self was unable and unwilling to grasp it, and she still expected me to be home any moment. By the time it began to dawn on her that this was really happening, the children had arrived home from school, blissfully unaware of the devastation in our lives. Denise's face told them that something was badly wrong, and looking down on her as she struggled to find the right way to tell them and to comfort them, I felt frustrated at my inability to support her, remembering how I had fought to find an easy way to talk to her in hospital and that too, had been in vain. Denise and I had spent a great deal of time talking about funerals and death on a daily basis, discussing our work as funeral directors and more recently as bereavement counsellors, so the subject was not foreign to the children. Although initially upset, made worse by the sight of their mother's distress, they soon acted "normally", giving all the indications of being immune to the feelings generally associated with bereavement. Their disbelief, however, was as genuine as Denise's but they assumed the recognised and acceptable image of 'putting a brave face on' for the sake of those around them. Denise, usually strong and positive for everyone else was desperate to regain that inner strength, but it eluded her now.

We have always had good neighbours, but typically, they were also too upset and confused to face Denise and whilst they would have liked to help, thought that they would be in the way, so decided to leave notes of condolence and flowers on the doorstep, to avoid upsetting them even more. Oh! How Denise would have welcomed their presence at this time, even if they were likely to say the wrong things. As evening approached and with little else that could be done that night, Denise retired early to bed, hoping to wake up next morning to find me lying in bed at her side, but distraught in the knowledge that this was not to be. She cried herself to sleep, frightened of what the future held for her, worried about the children, and desperate to know if I was alright.

She woke up several times during the night, and was desperately tired when morning finally came, bringing the memories of yesterday and no hope for the future. Luke and Jane, now teenagers, needed no waking for their routine enabled them to fend for themselves, and as if nothing had happened, they began the day as normal, fighting to be first in the bathroom and then organising their own breakfast. It was only when they were getting ready for college that they realised that their pretence at normality was futile. Suddenly they broke down and collapsed on the settee, Luke getting angry and Jane screaming uncontrollably. All Denise could do was to join them in their grief.

So now we are all on the wrong side of the fence, a side we have never experienced before and the fence is too high at the moment for anyone to see over.

It never occurred to me until now that I would not be given an opportunity to say goodbye to those I love so much. No chance to undo the things I regret doing and no opportunity to fulfil the unfulfilled. I am shouting now, but it is all in vain for no one can hear me any more. In spite of all the support I have given over the years to those grieving relatives I did not know, I despair at the prospect that I cannot comfort my own family in their grief. I feel guilty that I have caused all this and desperately sad that I have wasted so many opportunities during my life; opportunities to enrich the lives of those who now mourn my passing; I now curse the time I spent moaning at the children about their appearance, their table manners, their attitude, their not being the perfect human beings I wanted them to be. They are now left with the memories. Will they only remember the criticisms or will they accept that this is just a small part of my make-up, the part I dislike about myself the most? I wonder what they would say to me now if we all had just one more chance. I can see them and understand them, but I cannot touch them or communicate with them. I can no longer influence what they do or say. I cannot guide them even though I can now see the pitfalls clearly. I cannot wipe the tears from their eyes, ease their pain or turn their sorrow into happiness, but if thought transference were a tool in my possession, I would use it to instil a peace within their hearts and minds that would give them the strength to live on to achieve all that their dreams may enfold. Perhaps when I have learned to cope with my new existence, I shall find a way to lift them out of this black hole that is getting darker and deeper by the hour.

Although I can see them, it is a one way mirror, and their darkness is intensified by ignorance of my well being. They too, have so many things they want to say to me now but their thoughts are tinged with fear for my safety and panic about the unknown. Their limited faith in life after death may not sustain them, but it is too late to analyse what is right or wrong, for death has cheated them and happened prematurely in their eyes and they cannot think clearly about anything at present.

The doctor finally arrived at 11am. to offer his support, both as a medical practitioner and as a colleague with whom we had worked over many years. He prescribed some sleeping tablets for Denise but there was little else he could do. Friends were arriving at various intervals during the day, armed with flowers and kind expressions of sympathy, but each visitor unwittingly "twisted the knife" as the pain intensified and the reality of what was happening, began to dawn. Luke looked after his mother as best as he could that day, but Jane was distant and sullen. At midday, the Coroner's officer arrived to see Denise but she was in no fit state to answer his questions and they abandoned the interview until the next day. Knowing him and working with him should have made it easier, but as soon as she saw him arrive it was just more proof that I was dead, and at that moment, Denise was looking to wake up from the nightmare.

To Shed A Light

If purgatory is this state of being able to analyse my past and recognise all the areas of regret, with no opportunity to influence any changes - by way of compensation, - then what must hell be like? In these initial stages of my "after life" I feel cocooned and only able to concentrate my thoughts on the devastation I have left behind and all the guilt that this generates. These feelings are as real now as they have ever been but I have lost the power to control them. If Denise knew that I was able to share in her sorrow, she would be comforted but she knows nothing of my new existence or my frustration. No longer needing food for sustenance myself, I was surprised by the effect that lack of food was having on Denise. I was willing her to look after herself but it was to no avail. All she wanted to do was sleep and thus have another opportunity to wake from the nightmare to reality, but sleep evaded her too. She was reluctant to take the tablets that the doctor had left for her, but eventually she succumbed. She had no sense of time, with day drifting into night, darkness into light, and still no hint that tomorrow might be better than today and no restful sleep to compensate for her restless mind.

I am unable to describe my appearance for in my present state I am only aware of what is happening in the life that I have just left and everything else is just a haze, but looking at the shell I have vacated I am unhappy with the way that my body is now being treated. A hospital mortuary is as depressing as everyone imagines it to be and the vision of someone lying in a refrigerated cabinet alongside others who have also died is as real now for me as it has always been for others I have seen in my lifetime, and I find the experience distressing. It is not that I am physically affected by it, because I can feel nothing of the cold, and the embarrassment of lying naked on a metal tray is not so important either, but the thought that no-one any longer cares about where I am or what I look like, does matter. In reality, of course, the people who care about me have chosen not to think too deeply about my whereabouts at the moment because they cannot influence that anyway. The thought of my being in the 'hospital chapel' will be a source of comfort to them, although if Denise thinks about it she will know perfectly well where I am and also understand that there is absolutely nothing she can do about

To Shed A Light

it. Having been rolled out of the refrigerator and wheeled into the post-mortem room I now have to watch the autopsy being carried out upon my body. As an embalmer, I have been used to seeing the results of an autopsy on a regular basis but my task has always been to try and present the deceased in a way which is going to be pleasurable for the bereaved. That exercise is a far cry from watching the mortician dispose of his rubber gloves by slinging them into my rib cage just prior to suturing me back up again. And those sutures! Do they have to be so clumsily and quickly done? I guess I knew that they would want to examine my brain too, but to see him putting my brain in the trunk of my body and stuffing my now empty head with cotton wool and paper to soak up the blood just emphasises the fact that death is a great leveller, and that no-one, rich or poor, famous or not, pauper or prince, can escape this treatment.

Back in the refrigerator now, I analyse my appearance. My hair is wet and not in the right style at all. My features have now been distorted by the suturing of my neck and I have not been shaven. My nose has been stuffed with cotton wool and there is evidence of blood from the autopsy. My hands are still wet and the skin wrinkled as if I have spent too long in the bath, but my fingernails are bloody too. Most of my injuries were internal, but there are cuts, bruises and grazes everywhere and quite a deep gash in my forehead. I wonder why they did not suture that, but then, they never do. I hope my family does not see me looking like this, and yet I know that Denise will not care what I look like, as long as she has her opportunity to say goodbye. Now I look at myself and realise for the first time that the real me is not lying there. The real me is the one watching, the one that no-one else can see, the part of me that will always be loved and cherished by those who have always been there for me. So in a way, it is good that my personality has left its shell and the stuffed carcass is no longer required. The marks and scars are superficial for the part of me that Denise bids farewell to is still as clear in her mind as she is to me, and in that sense at least, nothing is lost!

The cause of my death now established there would be an inquest to decide how it happened because of the circumstances. It now occurs to me for the first time that the driver of the vehicle involved in my accident has also had a few sleepless

To Shed A Light

nights. Even the innocents are victims in these circumstances and in the absence of any witnesses he will be left to try and prove that he could not have avoided me. No doubt he will have to attend court too. Perhaps Denise will be spared the trauma of having to attend that, but that is weeks away. At some point prior to that my body will be disposed of but in the meantime I remain in my cold environment awaiting collection.

Chapter Three

A few months prior to my death saw the introduction of a couple of "Charters" for the bereaved, published in first draft form by two different like minded groups who were keen to improve the quality of funerals, one of which, the better of the two, asked for constructive criticism and I had been particularly keen to analyse the details of this one with a view to influencing the final draft, being unhappy with some of the proposals. Bob Pritchett, who has been a friend for many years also read my copy of the charter but looked at it from a layman's point of view, and was therefore not as unhappy with the content as I was. Although he was aware of the concerns I had we never really had the opportunity to discuss them in any detail, partly because he was often too busy, and then I became ill. My death finally put paid to any further discussion on the issue and in fact I thought it had been filed to the waste paper basket. However, Bob had also become interested in the charter and had studied it in great detail and was convinced that the draft needed no amendments. He was particularly impressed with the proposal that every bereaved person should have appointed a funeral guardian to look after the arrangements for the funeral and thus take away the burden from the nearest relative when they are too upset to cope.

Bob is a likeable chap, retired early from the bank where he had worked as a teller for almost all of his adult life and now with plenty of time on his hands. I have always enjoyed his company even though on occasion have found his manner a bit overpowering. He loves to get his own way, is stubborn and a little quick tempered but kind hearted and always eager to please. He is the sort of person who I would have labelled as being chairman of some political party and yet politics was something he never mentioned. I once heard him telling a colleague of mine that he was an agnostic, the only time I have ever heard him mention religion and even then he refused to elaborate. As far as he was concerned, religion and

19

To Shed A Light

politics were the two subjects that ruined friendships and should therefore never be discussed. He had been married before I knew him but it had only lasted a matter of months. There were no children and it was obviously painful for him to think about it, so we never spoke about it but I cannot help thinking that for him, this was his first real bereavement. Both his parents have since died, but he was not close to either of them and only ever speaks about them if he is trying to comfort someone else in their sadness. Then he will talk about how he understands because of the bereavements he has suffered.

He lives only a short distance from our home. I still think of it as my home as well and yet I suppose it is now Denise's house. It will not be 'home' again until she renews her stamp upon it because it contains too many painful memories at present, or perhaps that is just my inability to accept that our home can be as happy without me as it was when we were together?

Bob arrived on the doorstep at a point when Denise was at her lowest ebb. She had reluctantly taken the tablets that had been prescribed for her, had a gin and tonic and gone to bed. No visitors were really welcome at that point and Bob's timing was never brilliant. In spite of everything, Denise was pleased to see him and at least felt that here was someone she could talk to and his offer of help was sincere and appreciated. There were some practical things to be sorted out and Denise was not up to dealing with any of them so for once she allowed herself the luxury of accepting help from someone. He tried to tempt her with some food but she thought he was a bit too optimistic there. She looked drained and was obviously not coping anywhere near as well as I thought she would. Bob was carrying his briefcase, the first time I had seen him with it since his retirement and I wondered what it contained. Finances were not a problem so if he is going to try and sort her finances out, he will get short change from Denise. It was ages before he opened his briefcase but when he did I was dumbfounded. He produced the Charter that he was so familiar with by now and suggested that it would be a good idea if he saved Denise all the heartache of making the funeral arrangements and allowed him to act on her behalf, just as the charter suggests. What could she say? The offer was genuine, and he had obviously familiarised himself with all that was involved and there was no reason why she should say no. In fact she couldn't care less at that point and allowed him to guide her through the details, taking very little in at the time. An hour later and she was back in bed and Bob was off to see the Coroner to sort out the details.

Bob soon established that my death was straightforward and that although there was to be a full inquest, it was to be opened and then adjourned for the funeral to take place. He was unfamiliar with the procedure however. When his parents died, the certificates in both cases had been obtained from the hospital, so Bob followed the same pattern this time. He was surprised to find when he arrived at the casualty department that they had no idea what he was talking about and directed him towards the bereavement officer for further guidance. She was unable to give him the certificate either because the Coroner was involved but his journey was not entirely wasted. At least the bereavement officer was able to point him in the right direction and when he explained the circumstances and how he had become involved, she gave him a list of things he needed to accomplish. She recommended a funeral director just a short distance away from the hospital, but because by now the time was getting on, he decided to wait until the next day before visiting them. The truth is, that although he was keen to help, he did not cherish the thought of visiting a funeral director and was worried that it might bring back all the memories of his father's funeral which in all honesty had not gone all that smoothly. As he strolled back to Denise's home he reflected on the funeral and the problems he had had with his mother. The vicar, he remembered, was ten minutes late getting to the crematorium and then it was not the same vicar that had visited his mother prior to the funeral. He never did get to the bottom of that but determined that my funeral was going to be better. Denise was still asleep when he arrived, but Luke was there, so he just left a message to say that all was well and left it that he would get back to her the next day and went off home feeling pleased with the day's events.

To Shed A Light

Friends and relatives by now, were beginning to wonder when the funeral was to take place but once assured that the arrangements were now being looked after by Bob, felt happy in the knowledge that Denise was being well cared for. Denise too, was able to rest more easily because she had not been looking forward to dealing with the funeral arrangements.

Arranging the funeral the next day was not as easy as Bob had anticipated. He had arrived at Barklett's funeral service at about eleven o clock and was shown through to a waiting room which at the time was occupied by a young couple who were incredibly upset, having just visited the chapel of rest to see their baby. Before Bob could be seen he was joined by another set of grieving mourners who had also come to arrange a funeral. He realised that they were busy and was beginning to feel uncomfortable when a lady came in and beckoned him to follow her into another room. She apologised for the fact that he had been kept waiting, blaming the 'flu' epidemic for the rush and looked relieved to have a seat herself whilst arranging the funeral. As they were busy, there was a shortage of times available at the crematorium and it was obvious that it would be several days before the funeral could be fitted in. The duty minister at the crematorium was to try and visit Denise prior to the funeral but at least he had her telephone number in case he was unable to make it. There were a few questions that Bob found difficult to answer too. When his parents died, his brother had dealt with the arrangements and therefore these questions had not arisen before. What was to happen to my ashes, for instance? Well it was established that most people opt for scattering on the garden of remembrance at the crematorium and as Bob couldn't think of a better option, this was agreed. After all, Denise could always change this if it was a problem. The most difficult choice was the style of coffin. He did find this aspect upsetting and I must say that I was not too chuffed myself. Watching someone select a coffin for you is quite eerie really but I could not influence his choice and therefore ended up with something that was far more elaborate than I really wanted. Bob thought that hymns were a waste of time too, because of his agnostic tendencies, so he suggested some music to be played on the organ but as the crematorium organist was off

To Shed A Light

sick, he settled for some taped music instead. Bob chose a blue shroud to have me dressed in, and although that was an improvement on my present naked state, I would have preferred to be dressed in my own clothes. Bob thought he was pushing his luck when asking for a limousine. The transport was obviously spoken for that day, so he settled for just the hearse, with everyone using their own cars to meet the hearse at the crematorium. That would give him an opportunity to take Denise in the comfort of his own car and not have to worry about official cars. The funeral director thought that in the circumstances it was unwise to "view the remains" and felt that it was best for people to remember me as I was before the accident. There were several forms to complete, which all seemed a bit unnecessary but eventually the formalities were over. As an afterthought it was agreed that donations for a Cancer charity was better than having flowers and so the funeral director drafted a notice for the newspapers which were to appear in the next issue. After a while, it was decided that enough had been achieved for one day, and Bob left Barklett's and went home. He briefly rang to speak to Denise but was only able to speak to Jane this time so just said that the funeral had been arranged for two-o clock next Friday afternoon, details to follow after dinner, and set about cooking himself a meal. He had achieved a lot that day and was pleased to be at home for the evening. As Denise was still drugged he decided to go and visit her the next day. He had an early night and was still making plans for the next day as he drifted off to sleep. If only Denise could have the luxury of a peaceful night's sleep, but she tossed and turned and felt generally uneasy. Part of her was too tired to care and eventually that part won and she drifted in and out of a restless sleep for the remainder of the night. I do not sleep in my new existence and to some extent this is a bonus because I can re-live all the happy memories without being hindered by sleep but so far most of my time has been spent in turmoil and frustration with little time to reflect on what has been good in my life. There must be a way of influencing what is happening to my family, but I have yet to find the means and I am now looking at Bob and Denise in their different environments, who are at this moment in time, both

To Shed A Light

fast asleep and blissfully unaware of the problems that lie ahead.

As far as Denise is concerned, she is content that the arrangements for the funeral are being looked after and as the thought of even going out at the moment fills her with dread, the fact that a friend has lifted this burden from her, enables her to rest more easily. Her dreams are still tainted with despair, her waking moments a constant analysis of the past life we had together, but because of her reluctance to accept the fact that I have died, her willingness and ability to organise the practicalities of living has deteriorated dramatically, to the point where she has to rely on Luke, Jane and the likes of Bob to do the things which she would normally be so good at.

Bob in his bed now, rests his weary bones, having worked them harder in the last few days than at any time since leaving the bank and the responsibility of organising the funeral is taking its toll, mentally. He still has much to do but will wake refreshed and eager to continue his supportive role. In contrast, Denise will wake up to a day that holds the same fears and misery, for the little sleep she has, changes nothing.

Bob was in the middle of shaving when the telephone rang shortly after eight thirty in the morning. It was the coroner's officer calling to check how Bob was getting on. On hearing what arrangements had been made, he agreed to organise the appropriate certificate for cremation, but expressed surprise that it was to be a cremation as he knew me fairly well and had always been under the impression that I favoured burial. Bob, having been advised by the funeral director that eighty per cent of funerals are now cremations, decided that this was the right thing to organise but it occurred to him now that he had not actually discussed that point with Denise, or if it comes to that, any other aspect of the arrangements. What Bob has organised is what Bob would want for himself and he had not until now, realised that my wishes might be different to his own. Nevertheless, he was confident that all was well and decided to visit Denise later in the morning and confirm all the arrangements. He was actually getting ready to leave the house, when a distraught and irate Denise telephoned. Her newspaper had been delivered and she could not believe the arrangements that were reported. As Bob was in the throws of leaving the house anyway, she decided to wait until he arrived before going through her list of problems.

If anything was likely to help motivate Denise, it was the realisation that the funeral arrangements were not as she had expected. In the first place, why had Bob gone to Barklett's funeral service when both she and I had worked for Donald Henshaw's funeral directors for the best part of twenty years? Why having got that wrong was it compounded by arrangements for cremation instead of burial and donations instead of flowers? This information she had gleaned from the death notice in the newspaper but when she met with Bob she also found out that there were no arrangements for her to see me before the funeral, no church service or hymns, no opportunity to follow the hearse from home in a limousine, an inappropriate choice of coffin and a dressing gown instead of my own clothes to dress me in! Looking on, as I am, I can understand how Bob has arrived at the decisions he has but they are so far adrift from what Denise was expecting that nothing short of rearranging the entire funeral is going to satisfy her. There are certain decisions that are made at this sad time in order to address the needs of the bereaved and some, solely on the grounds that they will satisfy the pre-determined wishes of the person who has died. One of the most fundamental of those decisions is whether to opt for burial or cremation and there need be no logic exercised to determine which is best. For some, it is simply a gut feeling one way or the other, for others it may be for religious reasons whilst others will find one method or another distasteful, inadequate, repulsive, expensive or a host of other adjectives you can think of. The point is, that the decision is a very personal one and sometimes individuals feel strongly one way or the other, and may even hold differing views to their spouse or partner. My own views are well known to Denise, because we have not only spoken many times about our funeral, but also planned some of the arrangements. Had Bob thought to ask, or if Denise had been sufficiently 'with it' at the time to remember, my last will and testament details my own funeral requirements and includes the information relating to the grave which we purchased many years ago in the cemetery in

To Shed A Light

the town where we live in order to ensure that I would not be cremated. My reasons for choosing burial are not based on logic or religion but I find it difficult to find the words which adequately describe how strongly I feel about it, and I would be mortified, if that is still possible in my new state, if this particular wish is not granted. In my will I have also stated the name of the funeral director to use. I have worked for Henshaw's for many years and know that above all else, they will look after Denise and take good care of me. However, while Denise and Bob discuss the problem, life goes on, and I now watch my body being pulled out of the refrigerator and plonked unceremoniously into a fibre glass coffin by two of the scruffiest individuals you could imagine. Trundled along on a trolley to the waiting estate car I am then driven back to Barklett's. I should be pleased that at least I have been taken out of that wretched cold room but Bob did not see beyond the office at Barklett's and it is not very impressive. My body stayed in that fibreglass coffin for the rest of the day, either because they had no staff available to take me out, or because they had nowhere satisfactory to leave me. When I was eventually transferred to a different room, I was thankful that it was not a refrigerator although I cannot help thinking that I was just another body!

Within minutes of speaking to Denise, Bob was aware of the problems he had caused but being conscious of the fact that everything he did was all done for the right reasons did not help at all. My colleague, Adam, at Henshaw's was disappointed that Denise had chosen to go elsewhere to arrange the funeral, and in any other circumstances, would have been in touch to see if there was anything he could do, but he did not want to add salt to the wounds, and he was unaware in any case as to how the problem came about. Denise, however, was not just disappointed, she was livid! In fact there was no way anyone but Adam was going to do the funeral, whatever arrangements had been made but it was now complicated by the fact that the details had appeared in the newspaper. She also wanted to retain Bob's support because she was aware of the way he felt. The solution, as far as Denise was concerned, was to go to Henshaw's and see Adam and ask him if he would take over the arrangements and sort out the problems with Barklett's. Bob agreed to go with her for moral support but also appreciated that he was about to learn a few lessons about arranging a funeral. To break the ice, Denise telephoned Adam and briefly explained what had happened. She knew he would understand, and when she had finished her conversation with him I saw her smile for the first time since my death. I was pleased that anyone should work so hard on my behalf and then quickly wondered whether or not I was allowed to have those feelings now. At this point, Denise broke down again, but this time it was partly due to the relief she felt. This was to be her first time out of doors since my death and she was nervous about that too. She was not looking forward to meeting anyone and went to great lengths to ensure that no neighbours were around before venturing out to the car. Bob drove and the twenty-minute journey was conducted in silence. Denise was surprised at the way she felt about meeting her work colleagues in these different circumstances. Even the building as they approached as customers, took on a new image and she trembled as they walked into the reception. Bob would have preferred the floor to swallow him up at this point, but to his credit he braved it out and was immediately impressed by the difference in the surroundings. Adam was on the telephone so they were shown into the waiting room. Bob compared it with Barklett's and realised just how homely the atmosphere was here. Denise was upset as she looked around because in many ways it was like being at home. My stamp was on everything she looked at. The choice of wallpaper, drapes, light fittings and even the pictures on the wall had all been my choice and we had smiled at the time because I had organised it without reference to her about suitable colours. She was as impressed now as she had been at the time she first saw it, but I suppose she is biased too. As she sat there pondering, she realised that I was not at Henshaw's and she wondered where I was. It also crossed her mind that Barklett's are not going to be very pleased either. She was just daydreaming about the consequences of changing all the arrangements when Adam arrived and took them into his office. His voice was soft and his manner genuinely sincere but he too was upset and found the whole business very difficult. His telephone conversation had been with Barklett's and to say that they were being uncooperative is an understatement but Adam did not give Denise the impression that there was a problem. Adam had arranged to have my body transferred to Henshaw's and in fact that was taking place as they were speaking. Nathan and Herbert, who had been sent to collect me, also knew me well and the task was not made easier by the indignant staff at Barklett's. However this type of situation has happened before and no doubt will again in the future. They were disgusted at the way I had been dealt with, and in fact hardly recognised me. Dealing with someone they know is hard enough but to see that everything is not as perfect as they would have wished is disturbing. I wondered what steps they would take to improve my appearance before Denise saw me. In spite of the fact that I felt nothing, I was pleased to be handled with respect and could hear them talking about me as they drove back to their premises. They were referring to my good and bad points and I had to smile at the excuses they made for me in order to justify some of the things I had done, that at the time they were obviously unhappy about. It is odd how people normally avoid saying anything derogatory about the dead and yet during life we try harder to find the faults than we do the good points. Due to the state I was in, Adam decided not to let Denise know that I was being moved, so that it would give them an opportunity to do something about it, and after the fleeting thought in the waiting room about my whereabouts, Denise did not mention it. I was pleased to watch the 'quality procedure' in action, recording my details in the mortuary register and noted that they were making a special effort to ensure that they got everything absolutely right. I also noticed the grin on Nathan's face as he wrote it. I smiled too, because I would have done just the same in his position.

    Back in the office, the atmosphere has become less strained, and even Bob has started to relax. There was nothing to be gained by dwelling on the mistakes of yesterday, and Adam did not mention it. Naturally, he wanted to be certain that my wishes and Denise's thoughts were all catered for in the arrangements he makes and therefore he was more thorough than I have ever known him to be and this served to emphasise

To Shed A Light

for Bob just how different it can be when the correct questions are asked, but nothing else was said.

So this time a burial was arranged at Huntmoor Cemetery, just a mile away from home in the grave that we had purchased. It was to be organised so that there would be space in the grave for a second interment. Denise, whilst she had never been too fussed either way about being buried or cremated, had accepted that it was something that meant a great deal to me and had agreed to be buried too. The cemetery used to cater for the needs of the village, but the village grew into a town and space was limited, and thus grave spaces were being used more quickly than ever before. It was at this point that we decided to purchase a grave space in order that we could be buried there. We were fortunate too, in that we were able to select a grave by the path and we have often joked about the fact that we will be able to visit the grave without getting our feet wet. They eventually ran out of space and had to extend the cemetery. The next move will be to create a new cemetery elsewhere, for there is no adjoining land for an extension now. How many people will think to reserve a grave space before it is too late? How many would even consider this to be something to think about in advance? When we are young or fit and healthy, the need to sit down and talk about funeral arrangements is seldom recognised. As we get older, we are more aware of the need, but less inclined to grasp the nettle and when we become ill it is not a subject that we feel able to approach. Sometimes a last will and testament is thought of and dealt with but mainly to address the desire to tidy up the finances, and the inclusion of comprehensive funeral instructions within the document is sadly, often overlooked. This lost opportunity frustrates the next of kin or executor who is relying on some pre-determined wishes for guidance in their duty to arrange a funeral which will represent the wishes of the person who has died and the family who are left. Expressing these desires is all well and good, but futile if no-one is aware that these instructions have been left, which is why Bob made such a 'pig's ear' of the arrangements. Knowing someone intimately, solves the problem to some extent, and it was inevitable that Denise would eventually realise that her wishes and also mine, were not being addressed. The role, therefore, of a funeral guardian to look after the bereaved and take over the task of arranging the funeral, as suggested in the charter, could fall down if this representative is acting alone. No-one doubts their motives, but in reality, there is one unavoidable matter which cannot be solved by the help of a third party who is divorced from the pain and suffering of the bereavement. I refer to the need to be involved with the actual arrangements, as upsetting as this might be. Too often we try to shield the next of kin from the distress of arranging the funeral, assuming that the task of choosing a coffin, organising transport, deciding on whether or not to visit the chapel of rest, and all the other decisions that are made, are beyond the capability of someone who is so upset. Funerals are upsetting! To look back after the funeral in the knowledge that everything went well because of the care and effort involved is a great source of comfort to the bereaved, long after the 'guardian' has gone back to his or her normal way of life. The realisation, in contrast, that something of great importance to the next of kin has been missed because the question was never asked, or was answered incorrectly on their behalf, can be regretted for many years and yet may have been so easily accomplished. Bob knew that I disagreed with this aspect of the charter but he never viewed it in the same light. I know now that he wishes he had acted as a support rather than a mouthpiece but I do not blame him for the mistakes he has made.

    At this point, Claire brought in a cup of coffee, but somehow, the nicer people are, the more emotional one becomes and Denise broke down again. This in turn started Claire off, which enabled Denise to control her emotions, and she regained her composure. This need to put on the right 'face' for the outside world is a major problem and whilst Claire was not embarrassed, nor Denise for that matter, this was the first time she had deliberately tried to control her emotions for the sake of someone else. She knew that this would not be the last occasion when she would feel the need to do that. Denise asked if they could just get to the stage where Adam had sufficient information to get provisional arrangements made, as she was exhausted by now and really wanted to complete the details the next day, once all the previous arrangements had been cancelled and the new ones put into effect. Adam simply established that there was to be a church service in the Church of England church opposite the cemetery and suggested a new date which would enable them to put a corrected notice in the newspapers in plenty of time and called it a day. There was no need for Denise to thank him as she did, for he knew how much she appreciated what he was doing. It was not in Bob's nature to apologise for anything really for he was the sort of person that found it rather humiliating to admit that he was wrong but Adam was not the type to expect an apology or to gloat either, so he made it easy for Bob to go home feeling better about the way things had turned out and he felt more comfortable now about his supportive role and thought that he could probably regain any Brownie points that he has lost.

Chapter Four

Denise could see the sun shining through the curtains when she awoke next morning, and in some small way it helped the start of her day. Yesterday had been so awful that she decided that it could not get any worse and thought for the sake of the children, they needed to see her in a more positive mode. When she explained to them what had happened and they realised that all was to be sorted out satisfactorily, they decided that I would have seen the funny side of it in different circumstances and this made Denise think more clearly about the way forward. The theory of bereavement counselling, so well known to Denise, suggests that there are stages of grief that one has to go through in order to come out at the other end but there is no set pattern or set of rules or guidelines to indicate how well or badly one is progressing. Invariably, people are surprised by the depth of feeling and the length of the grieving process and confused because the affect seems to be different for each individual. When we see the devastating affect that a death has on others, we never realise that it will be the same for us and we can always think of good reasons why we would be able to manage. This morning, Denise reflects on the past few days and accepts that for her too, it is worse than anything she could have imagined. I wish I could contact everyone and encourage them to send a card to her, because I know that the cards helped me when I was in hospital. I need not have worried, because when the postman arrived he delivered masses of condolence cards.

"Somebody's birthday?" he called through the letterbox. Denise did not answer but smiled through the window to him. He would find out soon enough and regret that impulsive remark. This reminded her to close the curtains upstairs and down to let neighbours and regular visitors know what had happened. She decided to dress in black to go and see Adam and would reserve judgement as to whether or not to continue wearing black after the funeral was over. Denise has a particular problem. The people she knows well are quite used to seeing her wear black because she wears it at work every day so they are less likely to realise that I have died, but the grapevine, the newspapers and the general gossip will bridge the gaps and before long, everyone will know. The hardest people to tell will be our own relatives and Denise is aware that this has yet to be done. She rang Bob, who would not have been surprised if he had been disowned from now on, but Denise was not one to hold a grudge and there was no reference to recent events when she spoke to him now. She got Bob to walk round to her house so that they could go together to Henshaw's and by ten-o clock they were on their way. Bob could see a change in Denise this morning, but thought it unwise to refer to the fact so merely accepted it. The familiar smell of fresh coffee greeted them as they entered the reception and it was not long before they were looking for a second cup. I now saw Bob smile for the first time as Denise asked for some more coffee. This was a side of her that he had not seen for some time. Adam was not in when they arrived and she realised that they should have let him know what time they were arriving. Claire asked if Denise minded if she carried on with the arrangements to save them waiting and I immediately noticed Bob's frown. He felt sure that she would wait for Adam to return and was taken aback when she agreed to see Claire instead. In truth, it mattered little who saw her, because everyone would have a part in making the funeral happen. They all had their own roles, but they also completed any unfinished arrangements no matter who had seen the family. After all, if Adam were to fall sick, my funeral would still have to go ahead. Whilst Bob was concerned that some of the questions might be missed, he need not have worried. Claire confirmed the details so far before moving on with the arrangements.

Although Denise was here for a second time in order to complete the details, it is true to say that the majority of funerals are arranged with only one visit. The church and the cemetery had been booked last night and so the rest of the details can now be addressed without the same degree of urgency. Denise felt quite relaxed about the delay before the funeral whereas some people by now would have expected the funeral to be over. It had been re-arranged for a week

To Shed A Light

hence at the same time of day. Claire now carried on with her questions. Bob was surprised how efficient she was and yet her manner was gentle and sincere. He realised the benefits of dealing with someone that you have known or at least met before and decided to follow this up with Denise afterwards. They were now talking about a brick grave, something that Bob had never heard of but something I was very keen to have. This was not in the will, but Denise wanted that to happen too. The delay prior to the funeral was planned to enable the grave to be prepared and the brickwork completed. Claire asked for permission to embalm my body and at this point I thought Bob was going to have apoplexy. Because Denise was so familiar with the request, having asked the same question many times herself, she agreed without the need for an explanation, but it was obvious that if Bob had been here alone, he would probably have said no. There is never a good time to discuss embalming with someone after the death has happened but it is extremely important. I have given many talks to groups of nurses, Rotarians and similar groups and have always included an explanation of embalming, the reasons for doing it, how it is achieved and the costs involved and there have generally been more questions relating to that aspect than to the funeral details.

I used to explain that embalming is really carried out whenever we want to preserve the body, albeit only temporarily. When the deceased dies in this country but the funeral is to take place abroad, it is important to ensure that nothing unpleasant happens to the body en-route. The airline regulations usually insist because of this, that the body be embalmed. Many families today enjoy holidays abroad, and some of the package tours make it extremely difficult or expensive to return prematurely. When a relative dies at home therefore and the next of kin or near relatives are away from home, we would embalm the body in order that the funeral can be delayed for a week or two, pending their return. It is also important to ensure that the body remains in or is restored to a sanitary condition. People die in all sorts of places and at the most inconvenient times. Sometimes they will not be found for some time and the resulting deterioration is incredibly upsetting for relatives. It is also more pleasant for funeral staff to work in an odour-free environment. The 'smell' associated with death, disappears once the body has been embalmed. The last and to some extent, the most important reason for embalming today, is to restore the appearance of the deceased to that just prior to death which ensures that the relatives' lasting memory is a pleasurable one. It is true to say that the embalming process is not a pleasant one. I am reminded of the operation that I had to remove the cancer from my intestine. Had I analysed the way in which that was to be achieved, I dare say I would have been reluctant to agree and yet my desire to be restored to good health again would have won, I am sure. Naturally we prefer not to think about the means to the end in these circumstances. Embalming is no different. The process, which if the death is straight forward and no post-mortem examination necessary, consists of injecting embalming fluid, which is a formalin-based fluid, into the arterial system, often using the Carotid or Femoral arteries, draining the blood at the same time from the corresponding vein. The fluid, which is often pink in colour, restores the natural colour of the skin, arrests decomposition and leaves the body in a sanitary condition. Once the organs have been emptied using a trocar, and treated with cavity fluid the process is complete and the final presentation can be carried out. This will involve dressing the deceased and shaving when necessary, cleaning the finger nails, closing the eyes and mouth and then if necessary, using a little make-up to improve the colour of the skin. Sometimes, a problem will exist, like arteriosclerosis, which will make it difficult if not impossible to get the embalming fluid to the extremities from one injection point. In these circumstances other arteries are used and their corresponding veins to ensure that the whole body is properly embalmed. Of course, the above process does not work when an autopsy is carried out, as the blood circulation is destroyed during the examination. As Claire has now excused herself so that she can give the embalmer instructions to embalm my body, I will describe that process as it happens. I am now used to the idea of being moved about and feel in a strange sort of way, that while I am being transferred from one area to another, for whatever reason, I am being looked after. I just wish that I could have been

To Shed A Light

transported from the hospital to Henshaw's direct in the first place, rather than via Barklett's, but at least Denise has not analysed that so far, and is therefore content with my present whereabouts.

So, here I am again, on a stainless steel tray, about to be embalmed. The suturing has now been undone and my organs transferred to some viscera bags, which will eventually be returned to my ribcage. The rubber gloves and newspaper, which had also found its way into my trunk, have now been discarded with all other clinical waste and I feel better about that. Some cavity fluid has been added to the viscera bags to preserve my organs and the embalmer is now injecting the embalming fluid into my legs, arms, head and trunk via the arteries that serve those areas, from within the ribcage. Any vessels, which were severed in the post - mortem examination, have been clamped to prevent the embalming fluid from seeping out elsewhere. Any blood or excess embalming fluid which has managed to find its way back into the trunk of my body, has now been aspirated and he is now replacing the viscera bags containing my organs within the body. He has laid a piece of wadding over the bags as a precaution, replaced the sternum and is now taking great care to suture my body back up again, ensuring that the sutures which are used in my neck are small enough not to be seen when I have been dressed again. Having done this many times myself, I appreciate the care he is taking and thankful that Denise will know nothing of the state I was in before. He has now washed and shaved me and I look much better than I did. I have been wondering what efforts Brian will make to deal with the gash in my face and the numerous bruises and scratches so I was pleased to see the cosmetics box at his side. Whilst I am not keen on the use of make-up to enhance the appearance of someone after death, there are circumstances, like my own, where it is the only way to disguise something that would otherwise be unpleasant to see. Brian has now melted some wax into the gash on my face and finished it off with some cosmetics to achieve a natural appearance. I think Denise will be pleased now and can rest assured that as far as this aspect is concerned, I have been well treated.

I have now been dressed in my own clothes, seldom worn casual cord trousers and an open neck shirt and cardigan. They can now discard my stuffy suits and ties, which I seem to have lived in for years.

Meanwhile, Denise and Bob have been continuing to reorganise the details of the funeral with Claire. While I have been explaining the embalming process, they have dealt with some other details which Bob had thought of as straight forward, only to find that yet more decisions have been reversed. Denise, Luke and Jane, at the very least, all want to see me before the funeral but there are others too who want to say goodbye to me in their own way. The chapel of rest at Henshaw's had been one of the first things to be changed when I first went to work for them and has been steadily improved since, such is the importance in my eyes, of making this area as homely and as welcoming as possible. It has become an ideal setting for friends and distant relatives and colleagues to pay their last respects, but whatever else it is, it is not home and for Denise the opportunity to have me at home again before the funeral is all important and had been routinely suggested by Claire, to the great surprise of Bob. If he was surprised at the suggestion, he was flabbergasted when Denise took up the idea. It was agreed to take me home for a couple of days before the funeral, which would give everybody else an opportunity to see me at Henshaw's between now and then. Bob could not see why anyone should want to see someone after death, let alone have them back home! He was there to support Denise but was staggered at just how differently the arrangements were being handled now in comparison with the experience that he had at Barklett's and he wondered whether we were being given special treatment because they knew us. I include myself here, for the care that I have received feels special too. I would be disappointed if I was not considered to be special by my colleagues, and Denise, Luke and Jane too have also all worked alongside them at some point and in a way also expect the best treatment. I am satisfied that if they treat us the same as any 'ordinary' customers are treated, we will still receive the best service, for we all learned a long while ago, that to do the best for someone at this time is the only approach. The little personal touches can be achieved for every client and thus no two funerals are the same and are therefore all special to the bereaved. Funeral staff have a unique opportunity to demonstrate that they care.

Denise had wanted the funeral to start from her home anyway, but Bob realised now that because I was going to be taken home, the funeral would have to start from there. Denise smiled knowingly at Bob and he returned a submissive grin. He also realised that she would probably want limousines now too and it seemed just a few moments later when Denise was suggesting two cars for the family. Had it not been for the fact that Bob genuinely felt that he was helping her by his mere presence, for she certainly appreciated his support, he would have gone home at this point. It is quite demoralising for the likes of Bob to watch all his plans disintegrate gradually, made worse because the changes are so dramatic. He expected them to be tweaked a little, but now he did not recognise them at all as being those he had organised. They were now talking about the church service, which also added salt to his wounds. Denise really does not know what to believe for the best, so she sympathises with Bob's agnostic views, but stops short of attaching a label to her beliefs or prejudices, conscious of the fact that in this regard she is carrying out my wishes. Religion is a subject that we have not talked about that much, but we were married in church and felt comfortable with that. It is true to say that we have been to church together since, but only on rare occasions. One thing I am certain about. Whatever decision she makes regarding the service arrangements for the funeral will have no bearing on what happens to me now. If Bob's arrangements had stood unchanged, I would still be where I am, not influenced by the whims of those left behind. Yet it is those who are left behind that are going to benefit most from the decisions that are made regarding the ceremony. If anyone doubts the wisdom of getting to know the funeral director before his services are required, few will say that there is nothing to be gained from meeting the person who is going to officiate at the funeral ceremony. Conducting the ceremony, in whatever capacity, is just an everyday task. It is a job which can be done well or badly by those who are trusted with the responsibility and they will be either keen to make an impression and support the family, or indifferent in their approach to the occasion. I have attended several funerals for members of my own family recently and have analysed the services, as one does in a professional capacity even when there for totally different reasons, and have been delighted with some and disgusted with others. In all cases, the vicar or priest visited the next of kin and noted the information that would be helpful in compiling the details for the service, and yet in only one case, was there any evidence of that on the day. Too frequently my relatives and friends came away from the services, uncertain as to whether they had attended the right funeral because the name of the deceased had not been mentioned, and the details given by the family have not been included either. The majority of people expect to gain something from the service, which will be a source of comfort for the future so they are naturally disappointed when it fails them in this respect.

It was as Denise began to analyse the arrangements for the church, that she realised that she had taken an important aspect for granted. Until now, Claire had assumed that the incumbent from Huntmoor Parish Church should be asked to conduct the service, whereas it is vital that Reverend Borin Worban, the minister who visited me so often while I was in hospital, officiates at my funeral. He has been an important part of my life and if my funeral is to mean anything it must relate to the life I have led and to exclude him would be disastrous. This is not a reflection on the Huntmoor vicar who has also known me for some time, because our association has been on a purely professional basis. My friendship with Brin is quite different.

I first met Brin about eighteen years ago. He had just started a new parish and I had just started work as manager at Henshaw's. I was looking to make my mark as a funeral director and he as a minister. I was impressed with the way in which he conducted a funeral service. Whether in church or at the cemetery or crematorium, he took the time to talk about the person who had died and no two funerals were the same. If ever I telephoned him with any information, he would include it in the service and over a period of time, our respect for each other grew. His wife, Nicky was also friendly, and I never felt as if I was talking to the vicar or the vicar's wife and we gradually became friends. After a while, because of his natural ability and willingness to care for the family at each funeral he conducted, I would contact him whenever I was stuck for a minister or where I felt his special qualities were called for, whether or not the bereaved lived in his parish. He rarely declined, but on several occasions the circumstances were complicated or tragic. On at least two of these funerals we had to deal with the collapse and subsequent deaths of two of the mourners at the funeral, and he had ended up giving mouth to mouth resuscitation whilst I telephoned for the emergency services. He invited me to talk, as a funeral director, to a group in his church, and that was one of the first talks I had ever given in public. He eventually left the parish and I lost touch with him for a while, even though his move had only taken him about twenty miles away, but into an area where we never worked. It was some years later, now about eleven years ago, when Brin heard that I was in hospital about a mile away from where he was ministering and our friendship was renewed. He had supported Denise throughout, much of which I was unaware of until I had been discharged. There was therefore, no question about who should be leading the funeral service.

Chapter Five

Throughout my career I have met people from all walks of life with differing views on religion and different interpretations on the ritual to be adopted for the funeral service. My own views simply add to the confusion, but it emphasises the need to address the wishes of those who have died, in a way that will enhance the ceremony for those who are left. I am sure that Borin will do justice to my cause in this respect, and trust that it will not conflict with his desire to perform as a devout member of the Church of England where the form of service is laid down. I do not believe that I will suddenly shoot towards heaven, be immediately cast into hell or remain in this state of limbo if Borin gets it wrong, but I do think that there will be some very unhappy mourners around who will criticise him if he fails to get the balance right. The ceremony would normally last about twenty minutes if it ran true to form, of which five minutes would be spent talking about me and the other quarter of an hour singing hymns that no-one recognised, listening to an extract of one of the "appropriate" readings from the Bible and sharing in the prayers that would please some and offend others. If Borin were to fall ill and his place taken by another vicar, then the five minute tribute to me would consist of whatever information he could glean from Denise in the time available. Those members of the congregation who because of their line of work, attend many funerals, would not be surprised at the impersonality of the ceremony for they would liken it to the service at the crematorium when taken by a 'duty' minister and which leaves everyone wishing they had stayed at home. Yes, I want my funeral service to be held in church because for me it is the appropriate place. This is not because I am a good Christian, or because I am a regular churchgoer or because it will right any wrongs that I have done. In spite of the life I have led, and I am sure that the best I can hope for as an epitaph on my tombstone will be, "he meant well", I am thinking now of the pleasure that can be afforded to all those I love and care for when given the opportunity to say goodbye to me in an atmosphere of dignity and tranquillity in the knowledge that no-one is going to hustle them out of the building because there is another funeral waiting. Unless there is still time for miracles, there will also be ample room in the church for all those who would wish to attend my funeral, but if for a variety of reasons there are only sufficient mourners to fill the first pew, it will still be the right place to hold the service. As the burial is to take place just fifty yards away from the church, it is also the most practical option because there is no cemetery chapel there, but I always find them impersonal places for a service anyway and so I am pleased with these arrangements so far. If my wishes are granted, instead of the usual twenty minutes, the service will last about an hour and there will be something for everyone as a source of comfort. The atmosphere should be relaxed with no one feeling offended because the ceremony is different to 'normal'. As I am unique so should my service be a "one-off" and this is true for everyone. The mourners will go home knowing exactly whose funeral they have attended and they will be lifted by that part of the ceremony that is most appropriate for them as individuals.

It is not unusual to have a service without any religious content at all and I have led the ceremony, as a funeral director, on a couple of occasions although I did not feel comfortable at the time. Planning the service is time consuming and for me it led to many sleepless nights between the time of death and the time of the funeral. Whilst it may be inappropriate or hypercritical to have a Christian service for the non-believer, I do know of many people who are embarrassed by Christianity and who would certainly never admit to having a faith, and can therefore give their family and friends the impression that a religious ceremony is not wanted. I liken it to the person who says: "You can put me in a plastic bag when I am buried," but secretly hopes that no-one will. Others feel that to have a religious service is like having an insurance policy. They are not really sure whether they should have one or not, so they err on the side of caution and arrange for the vicar to be there just in case.

To Shed A Light

The music that is chosen for any funeral is as important as the words that are spoken. There can be a depth of feeling when listening to a piece of music which is far more meaningful to those who can associate it with the person who has died than perhaps the words of introduction which are often unfamiliar. With the possible exception of jazz music, which is just as suitable for the enthusiast, there is no music that I would be unhappy with. Denise and I have similar tastes in music and I am delighted that I did not specify anything in my will that would have prevented her from choosing what she would most like to hear as everyone is entering the church. With luck, the music will not stop immediately the last person is seated but will continue just long enough for everyone to realise that this is a very special part of the service and sets the atmosphere for the remainder of the ceremony. Music encourages reflection, which is another important aspect when saying goodbye to someone. I would prefer to listen to a string quartet, rather than the organ for this type of music and reserve the organ for the hymns that will come later. My service would continue with some sentences of scripture because I want the Christian burial service to be an important part, but not necessarily the dominant part of the ceremony. So I want the religious content to be 'sprinkled' throughout the service as a constant reminder of the reason for being there, without it being so heavily emphasised that it is a 'turn-off' for those who would prefer not to have it at all. The theme for the service would be me! This may sound arrogant, but it is one time in my life when the whole occasion is dependant on my being there, if only in spirit. Just like the smattering of Christian messages throughout, the service should show a picture of my life from the beginning to the end, to include some things that we might regret and some that have been a source of great joy, incorporating some of the failures and the successes of my life, because this is what makes up the real me. Every opportunity to smile, cry, or even laugh out loud should not be offensive, for if we do not feel comfortable about expressing all of those emotions in God's earthly home, where can we?

I was brought up, as many of us were in my neighbourhood in the fifties, with the idea that you had to be quiet in church.

To Shed A Light

Parents took their children outside if they dared to behave inappropriately, and that was before the service had started! There were no toilets of course, and yet we seem to have survived for half a century without them in these buildings which are often too large to heat, where many of those attending funerals are quite old and usually incredibly upset. It is no wonder that nowadays there is an inherent unease about entering the house of God.

In order to enhance the service, therefore, it has to be planned, which is why the planning should perhaps be done before the death occurs. It is an easy matter to achieve once the idea has been germinated, but sadly, we do not do it. We wait until the need arises when we are not only too upset to think clearly about it but we have lost the opportunity to find out what is required from the very person whose life will be depicted during the ceremony. It is as if by thinking about our future needs in this respect we imagine that we will hasten our demise! We are much more likely to ensure that we can pay for it, often taking out pre-payment funeral plans to ease that particular burden, but that will do little to satisfy the needs of the bereaved, who will be looking for comfort from the funeral service when the death happens.

I am comfortable in my state of limbo where in my mind the time has not yet come where I satisfy the heavenly requirements but as yet, have not been confined to hell. Perhaps there is still the opportunity to redeem myself? I can reflect on my past, cursing the absurdities and reliving the happiest moments but can change nothing. The memories I have now of the life that I have lived would form the basis of the funeral service, for they represent the various facets of my life, which the mourners could relate to. At this moment in time, only I am aware of that, so my precise wishes are not likely to be met, but those who are closest to me are aware of the experiences that I have had which have helped to influence the person I have been. The service, as far as I am concerned, must represent the style of life that I lived but must put into context, the value of material things that, at the end of our time, are worthless. Death in this sense, is a great leveller. There are, as I and many of my colleagues have retorted in the past, "no pockets in a shroud". There are some gifts that we possess, however, that not even death can destroy. The influence we have on the people that are left is never destroyed and can be passed on to countless generations of unrelated people. This is an area that makes each individual unique, and which can be represented in the funeral service and does not have to be in itself, mind-blowing. The very fact that a particular quality is worthy of mention will ensure that the service is also unique and it is vital that it is not treated lightly by those who have the responsibility of incorporating it into the service. This is why, when a vicar tells his congregation, only those details that he has been asked to include, it sounds so insincere and artificial. The same thing voiced by someone who has shared the moment or the experience, is of far greater value and watching the congregation nodding their approval and their recognition of real memories is heart-rending but incredibly beneficial. Quite apart from actual memories of events that have been shared, close relatives often have years of dialogue to remind them of the years gone by and some of these fond memories have a much deeper meaning for the family. Regrets, heartache and times of trial are also part of someone's life and it would be hypercritical and unnecessary to avoid reference to some of these moments too, within the ceremony. Disability and strengths and weaknesses of character and personality are also ingredients that cannot be ignored. Glimpses of the past are often all that is necessary to impart the whole picture to the mourning congregation. Sitting in church listening to a tribute to someone's life, has many times in the past, been enlightening. One of the most difficult aspects of this desire to create an overall picture of someone's life is finding the speaker who is sufficiently close to the family to know from personal experience what has happened but who is also distant enough to be able to cope with the trauma of the occasion. Some of the most experienced public speakers have failed in this respect because it is impossible to remain unemotional at all times. But it does not have to be just one person. There are different people who can represent various stages of the deceased's life and if each can confine themselves to the experiences that they have shared, the service will be enriched by their input and will not put undue strain on any one person because they can keep it fairly short. There will of course be gaps in the history and no doubt some things which are best left unsaid.

I try to visualise from the memories I now have of my life, which I would include if I could write the text of my own tribute.

I had a happy childhood, and there is no doubt that some of these early experiences influenced my life in later years. The English teacher at my junior school, for instance, was never satisfied until I was in tears. Handwriting was her forte, but not in the earlier days, mine, but with her perseverance, whatever her motivation was, I developed my handwriting skills and became her star pupil. I retained that ability to write well throughout my life and have always been impressed with a well-written letter from others. Certainly I believed, quite wrongly of course, that anyone applying for a position with a hand-written letter of quality was almost bound to be suitable. I also spent time trying to show Luke and Jane how to write "properly", and although initially successful, they both found their own 'style' eventually. They I am sure would smile about that now. Life in general at the junior school gave me a false sense of security, because I got on well and believed that all schools were the same. Unlike my two brothers who did extremely well in their eleven plus examinations, I struggled, and although I passed, it was only for my second choice of school. With hindsight, it would probably have been better if I had failed the examination and gone to a Secondary Modern school where I might have been top of the class. As it was, my time at the grammar school was a nightmare from start to finish. Not badly behaved, just stupid! I detested the teachers, with the possible exception of one although I am not sure about him now, and he committed suicide when I was in the third year and my French and woodwork lessons deteriorated from then on. My reluctance to do homework, partly because I understood very little, meant that I was kept down a year and so had no opportunity to maintain any long-term school friends. Those in the lower form had been friends since they started school together, and I lost touch with those in the form I had to leave. I hated rugby football and remember having to play without boots once because they were dirty and with a towel round me on another occasion because I had forgotten my shorts. That humiliation has lived with me ever since. Doing gymnastics without plimsolls is equally painful but I never knew why I had to do that. I left school without any qualifications but learned a lot about life and people. I worked for a butcher on a part-time basis while I was at school and those were some of the happiest days of my life. I worked hard for very little money, in all weathers, delivering meat on a bicycle that was too big for me, with brakes that scarcely stopped the machine, but I always managed somehow and grew in strength. I befriended the butcher's son and we spent many happy hours together. It was convenient to carry on working for them when I left school, but my mother was never very happy about it. She always thought I was capable of doing something better than shop work. At the age of seventeen I passed my driving test and my mother encouraged me to apply for a driving job at the local funeral directors where they were advertising in their window. I applied, but I was too young to drive the limousines. Nevertheless, they offered me an apprenticeship that I was happy to accept and started a career that was to be a way of life from then on. My mother was dying from Cancer at the time, but I did not realise just how seriously ill she was. She died before I reached my eighteenth birthday and was buried by the company I was working for at the time. The experience of seeing her in the coffin left me thinking that more could have been done to improve her appearance. I felt no sadness at the time, and in fact it was twelve months later when my father put an 'in memoriam' notice in the newspaper that I went to pieces, but no one ever knew. It is difficult to talk to people about the way you feel, twelve months after the event. So I lived with that sadness all of my life.

My twin sister, Elaine and I and my two brothers, Garth and Kevin, have always been close, although not geographically. If I ever argued with them, I do not remember it.

There were times when I was envious of others who were earning far more than I was and the hours were long with little social life. Because of the nature of the work I grew old before my time, mentally. I was surrounded by other people's sadness everyday but worked with a man who was to become one of the best friends I ever had. He and his wife supported me through many a difficult time and we worked on and off for several years together. I left and tried my hand at numerous jobs, constantly thinking that the grass was always greener elsewhere, but always came back into the profession that I felt happiest in and from my early twenties, decided to make it my career. I studied hard to become qualified as an embalmer, and felt that despite my schooling, my Latin had actually helped me to learn the theory I needed. I then studied for my diploma in funeral directing and eventually, moved to Henshaw's where I progressed over a period of nearly twenty years from manager to become managing director.

Some parts of my life are hazy, but meeting Denise was like being born again. For the first time in years, here was someone who showed me how to enjoy myself. I would be happy, therefore, to think that my funeral service could reflect that part of my life that I have led since meeting Denise.

My character was obviously formed in those early days but with the exception of my secondary education, I would change very little. There are always things that we wish we had never done or said and things we wish we had, but the decisions we make, rightly or wrongly are made in the light of the information we have at the time. Looking back with regret, therefore, serves no purpose unless in my new existence I have the ability to erase the areas of regret in readiness for a new life without the unwanted baggage, but to date, that gift has evaded me.

I look back now at the first twenty years of my life and realise that some of the harder experiences were learned during this period. Working for several small family funeral directors, I endured long hours, low wages and often did thankless tasks, was on call most days, with little time for the leisure activities enjoyed by the few friends I had at that time and liaised most of the time with people who were upset. And yet I never resented it. I hardly ever compared my wages with those of my contemporaries and even if a little peeved at their take home pay, which was almost always higher than my gross earnings, I was happy and never grumbled about the nature of the job. Those friends who were earning more never seemed to be satisfied or content. To some extent, I enjoyed the mystique, because even my friends did not like to ask what I actually did. I always had to suffer the jokes. "People are dying to see you", and "that's a dead end job!" are two of the more common witticisms but their laughter seldom hid their embarrassment and I smiled at them, rather than the jokes.

The "Straight 8" Daimler limousines that I first drove were huge and I will always remember the thrill of being behind the wheel for the first time, scarcely able to see the mud wings from my driving position. I could almost walk into the back of the limousine without stooping but whilst they were a wonderfully practical vehicle for the job, what a lot of metal to wash every day! There were several of them too. I used to liken the polishing of the car to the painting of the Forth Bridge; as soon as you had finished it was time to start again! Not helped by the owner who would habitually run his finger along the mud wings to see if they were clean underneath and delight in being able to show why it must be done again. The limousines used for funeral work today are nowhere near as practical as those of yesteryear, but they can be washed and polished more quickly which came about thirty years too late for me.

Nevertheless, my earnings would not pay for any training and the course in embalming was financially out of reach. So I left the funeral trade and went to work for a glass manufacturer. The shift work never worried me and I enjoyed the challenge of a new job and the extra financial rewards it produced. It also enabled me to pay for my embalming course which I could do during the day when on the right shift. The job was comparatively easy, and there was plenty of time when, as long as the temperature of the glass was correct, I could read a book. So I studied the textbook on 'Practical Embalming', much to the amazement and to some extent, amusement of the other workers, who never really took it seriously. Nevertheless, I learned the theory, almost 'parrot fashion' and was able to pass the theory examination. The practical was taught by a local funeral director who also operated an embalming school and as I became more experienced, he paid me for any embalming I carried out for him, which covered his tutor's fees, and so I qualified. For the first time in my life I felt that I had achieved what my

To Shed A Light

schoolteachers had said was unattainable but had no desire to return to my grammar school to rub it in. I must have picked something up from my schooling, but they would never know and I enjoyed a degree of satisfaction from this.

The higher salary was attractive, but it was no substitute for the happiness I had experienced in the funeral service and I hankered for a return to what I was good at. The drop in salary was acceptable because I was then employed as an embalmer, a status I was unused to and was proud of, having earned the promotion.

Achieving the diploma in funeral directing was not to be easy. There was a feeling that if I qualified as a funeral director, I would leave and take my expertise elsewhere. My employer therefore, made it incredibly difficult for me to train. I was told so often that the tutorial study course, which was the means of learning this skill, was out of print, that I decided to contact the trade association direct, only to be told that it had never been out of print. Disappointed at the lack of support, I purchased the study course direct and studied without my employer's knowledge. A senior manager helped me and to gain experience, he made appointments with his relatives for me to go and arrange fictitious funerals. They played along and never hinted that there was anything artificial about the interview. I would go along to their house, introduce myself as a funeral director and they would explain about the death in the family and I would arrange the details as if it had really happened. Only once, fairly near the end of the interview, did his uncle fail to resist the temptation to test my sense of humour. "The person who was supposed to have died had a habit of poking the fire", he had said, "so would it be possible to put the poker in the coffin with him?" With the best will in the world I was unable to control myself and we all ended up laughing helplessly for ages. I never met them again, but I have always been grateful for the help that they gave me for they enabled me to pass the examination. When I left my employment, I was still being told that the study course was out of print. I delighted in telling him that I had qualified without his help.

This was only one of many occasions where I had left one employer and not immediately started with another, but

To Shed A Light

always I would have a job of sorts to tied me over until it was time to start work with another funeral director. All of these, and there were many in these early days of my working life, taught me a great deal about people. I lasted about three weeks during a hard snowy winter, working for a coal merchant. There were many 'firsts' during this period of my life and driving the lorry was one of them. It was relatively easy until it had been loaded, and then it was torture. I was fairly strong, thanks to those early butchering days when my workmates watched with delight as I struggled to carry hind quarters of beef from the delivery vehicle into the shop. It was all I could do to reach the hook safely, but I gradually became stronger. Nevertheless, it had never occurred to me that coke and coal, delivered in bags had first to be loaded onto the vehicle and a real shock to the system when I realised that I had to fill the bags too! Although I was a driver with a mate, it was the mate who carried the coal, and me. I remember standing underneath the coke hopper, poised with the open bag which was nearly as tall as me, waiting for the hundredweight of coke to fall into it. Controlling the moment with a foot control only made matters worse, because I invariably chose the wrong moment to operate it, lost my balance and ended up shovelling more into the bag off the floor than had ended up where it was supposed to. I knew it always took me longer to do that preparation, than it took the drivers of the other vehicles at the wharf, but they were patient and if ever they were angry, it never showed. I almost had to stand on the brakes to stop the wretched vehicle once it had been loaded and invariably overshot the delivery address because of the longer braking distance. Almost the final straw was when I had done just that, and then reversed twenty yards to save the longer carry with the coal. The driver of the Mini was none too pleased with the damage to his bonnet, but he must have been having apoplexy whilst sitting in it, watching me slowly bearing down on him with no escape. Skidding about in the snow with a bag of coke on my back and emptying it anywhere but the right place sealed my fate really. I decided to leave before they helped me on my way. It was years afterwards that I realised the logic, lost to me at the time, of having a spare coal sack as protection for the back when delivering a ton of coal. When

To Shed A Light

the customer counts the empty bags to confirm the delivery of the right quantity of coal, he counts those extra bags too. Delivery to several customers in a week created a nice little surplus for somebody, I guess.

I worked for other butchers too, also for short periods, and learned a few tricks of the trade there. Customer care in those days meant learning to speak in "backslang" to ensure that the correct price could be charged to each one. Naively, I thought that there were sound reasons for these different prices. It was only when staff seemed to change at holiday periods following a stock check that I realised something was wrong. The two butchers, working together, could identify those customers who they could overcharge and also those who they could not. As I turned round to the block to prepare the joint, so they would whisper in backslang the price I was to charge. They would explain that this was an easy way to teach me the prices, without the customer getting the impression that I was only learning the trade, and thus trust my judgement. It was also fun though, because they could say, "Kool the gels on the lrig", and only I would know that there was a girl with nice legs approaching. I was not there for long enough to become expert at anything, but I learned a lot which was to help me in later years, if only when doing the shopping!

During these early years, my love life left a lot to be desired. I remember a girl coming into the shop with her mother and I arranged a date with her. We had agreed to meet in the shop doorway that same evening, but as the bus I was on passed the shop, I noticed her waiting in the doorway with her mother and stayed on the bus. It never dawned on me that her mother might only be there until I arrived and I had visions of a date with the pair of them. Whenever I saw them approaching I hid in the back of the shop and the others covered for me. I left soon after that and never saw them again. I have often wondered what would have happened if I had kept the date.

As a single person, it was awkward when, back in the funeral trade, I was expected to be on call after hours, for I had left home and the lodgings where I lived was shared with others, making it impossible to get called out without disturbing everyone else. So it was agreed that whenever I was on duty, I was to stay in the bedsit above the funeral

To Shed A Light

premises. There was no television, a radio that crackled and no opportunity to go out for a newspaper, in case the telephone rang in my absence. On one occasion, I was so incredibly bored that I took the telephone off the hook and went to the newsagent a few doors away for a magazine, but they were long lonely nights when on duty without a companion, so I welcomed the calls in the early hours and was so alert that it was as if I were working a night shift. I was excited in those days about the drama associated with the violent deaths, of which there seemed to be many, for the sadness which the mourners were experiencing did not always register as it did in later years.

I was living in a room in a large Edwardian house with a private landlord. He used to collect the rent on a weekly basis, often my only visitor, for I was too ashamed of the surroundings to invite anyone along. The room was adequate for survival, consisting of a bed, wardrobe, and armchair and a sink unit, cooker and small table. I had to share the bathroom with the two girls who were lodging in the other rooms on the same floor. Their clothes were almost always drying on an airer above the bath and as I was too shy to move them, I was seldom able to have a decent bath. I was so fed up on one occasion that I decided to use the public baths. It was bad enough being provided with a towel with the City Council's name splattered all over it for all the world to see, but having the water measured into the bath by the attendant was even worse. The only way of altering the temperature was by calling the attendant who would then return with a huge key and add hot or cold as required. Needless to say, I made do with the initial six inches of tepid water and resolved to make that my first and last visit. How embarrassing! I left those digs soon after and went to live in the flat above the premises. This was a common occurrence amongst funeral directors, in fact for many the flat was a compulsory condition of accepting the work. Wearing my black jacket, waistcoat and pin stripe trousers was a novelty at first, and I almost lived in them. I enjoyed watching people's expression when they saw my attire. I am sure that I was a solicitor or bank official in their eyes for I am certain that funeral directing was the furthest thing from their minds. Either that or they were extremely good at avoiding the subject. With hindsight, I suppose it could easily be the latter.

Chapter Six

Denise has decided to ask five people to give their different tributes during the service, and these will reflect five totally different aspects of my life. Roy Crater has been asked to reflect on those earlier years that only he could relate to. He shared so much of my life from the age of seventeen and for over a decade we laughed about so many things. My funeral would not be complete without him. My family life has to be recorded during the service as being the most important part of my life. Those who have been close to me, realise that my family meant more to me than anything else, but my workmates will probably think that my work was my life. My fellow Rotarians will remember the countless hours spent in their company whilst my friends will wonder how I had time for any of those things with all my various hobbies. Our work has been demanding and enjoyable, but many a weekend has been enhanced because we have been able to look forward to sharing part of it with David and June Koaley. Good friends are few and far between and I have certainly found it more difficult than Denise to get close enough to people to enjoy true friendship. Through my work and my Rotary I got to know and become friendly with many people, but that is not quite the same. David and June were special to Denise and I, and David will enhance my funeral service now with his input.

I only ever introduced one new member into our Rotary club, because I always felt that it was important to introduce the right sort of person. Gary Hallroad was such a person and he also, coincidentally, supplied us with flowers for the funeral tributes we made. He has done well to live up to the glowing reputation that preceded him and I was proud to think that I had been a part of his becoming a member. His wife, Mary, was suitably wacky to make a fun foursome when we socialised, and he was pleased to accept Denise's invitation to speak as a Rotarian. Actually, that is not strictly true. He did not like to say no and was petrified at the thought of what he had committed himself to, but although felt privileged to be

To Shed A Light

asked he decided to suggest that Malcolm Tyler, should do it as the founder president. Another lamb to the slaughter was to be Denise's Uncle Henry, the only person with the ability and the sensitivity to portray the "family man" without breaking down. Though a good speaker, he too knew what he had agreed to and did not cherish the idea, for he had probably been closer to me than any other member of Denise's family. My own relatives were too close to me to do justice to the tribute. Paul Mahen, the chairman of Henshaw's who up until now had been conspicuous by his absence, has nipped in to the office while Denise and Bob were there confirming the arrangements and been coerced into adding the final touches to the service. As my boss for the best part of twenty years it is appropriate that he does this, but quite how he will be able to achieve it without becoming emotional, I have no idea. I try to put myself in his place, reversing the roles and know that I would not have the courage to do it, but he is a remarkable man. In many respects we were very much alike, but I lacked his brain, breeding and background. Nevertheless, together we had some remarkable ideas, many of which came to fruition and which he will refer to in his tribute. We will wait for the funeral to see how my early days, my Rotary involvement, my friendships, family and my work all come together to give a snapshot of my fifty years on this earth and to see what comfort can be gained from it all in the space of an hour or so.

This is the second attempt that Denise's uncle Henry has had at writing the notes for his tribute and it is now the early hours of the morning with little progress being made but a great amount of heartache and waste paper. His experience as a speaker at various functions in the past only serve as a contrast to the task ahead and every poignant thought emphasises the difficulty that faces him. I am tormented with frustration at my inability to help and find it difficult to comprehend the depth of feeling aroused by the hole I have apparently left by my premature departure. The words he can find but the courage to express them is another matter. His sadness is tinged with pleasure as he thinks of the woodturning I have done. At least he can look forward to a Christmas without wondering what shaped bowl he will receive or what to put in it. Without warning, he walked into the next room and analysed the details of the sewing box that I had made for his wife, Alice, one of my better attempts at woodworking, and studied it for some time with mixed feelings before returning to the task in hand. When he returned, it was with a new vigour as if the light had been switched on for the first time and he could see clearly now. My carvings, paintings, woodturnings and carpentry, however amateurish they may have been, were not only an important part of my life, they were an escape from the misery of bereavement that I had dealt with daily, and my way of relaxing and replenishing my batteries in readiness for a new week. Henry wanted to refer to this in his tribute and in smiling over the Christmas bowl production found a strength that enabled him to complete his notes, rehearse the words and adjust the timing, before retiring whilst there was still some darkness left. The following day he tested the success of his efforts on Alice, and decided that as she was in tears within moments of starting to read it, that it was probably the tear jerker it was inevitably going to be, but was also appropriate. He would practice reading it with self-control as often as he could until the moment came where it was for real. At that point, he could only do what he could, and hope for inspiration and guidance from somewhere, he knew not where.

 Paul Mahen was struggling with his thoughts too, but his task was different and in some ways, more difficult. Almost twenty years of daily contact is in itself impossible to portray in a few words but a flavour of how it had been is what he is trying to achieve. They were undeniably good years by anyone's standards, starting with a continuation of the traditions that had been handed down and a gradual introduction of new and subtle changes that would transform the business over two decades, with the stamp of more ambitious minds upon it than in previous years. It had been a privilege for me to be offered the position initially, a stranger to the Henshaw family, but because of a determination to do what I felt was right for the client, which I believed would, in turn, be right for the business, I was accepted. Despite the fact that throughout my time there, I was "just an employee", I felt as if I was part of the family and I enjoyed every moment of it. Perhaps that is why people get labelled with the "workaholic" label afforded to those who delight in spending every waking moment at the office, or working at home to keep pace with all that is happening in the business. For me, I just loved the work, and the nature of the job ensured that the hours of work were unsociable for all who were a part of it. Our wives were also a part of that life that demanded their sympathetic ear and sensitivity, especially when answering the telephone at home when the office telephones had been switched over for the night. An unspoken loyalty to the business existed with all who were involved; such was the importance of their role.

I use the past tense to describe their involvement, conscious of the fact that for them it still exists and I am envious of their continuing vocation, and even in this state, am tormented by the problems of delegation. The building still stands without my support and the staff are as efficient as ever. I will take consolation from that, for I am sure that it will be a reflection on my managerial skills of yesterday, if it all goes 'pear shaped' tomorrow!

From day one and for that matter, even now, I see everything that has happened and the influence that I have had, through the eyes of the client. My mother's death has helped me to address the issues which I might otherwise never have seen and believe to this day that her influence in my joining this profession was far from coincidental. Whether or not she was ill at the time, I have no idea, but the experience of that bereavement has effected my entire working life. I know that in looking at my work through customers' eyes, I became hypersensitive, and possibly lacked the commercial qualities that make good businessmen, great, but have no regrets now about this aspect. Paul too, has always played 'devil's advocate' to ensure that any improvement in performance or efficiency would not detract from the service we were trying to offer. Over twenty years, with support from the other board members, who were all family of course, the premises, vehicles, staff, and overall service were enhanced with new aspects to the business to compliment the existing service. The introduction of a florists department coincided with the expansion of the business, as we took over a redundant church and turned it into a funeral home in a nearby town. This venture was tremendously exciting and the planning of this was as wonderful as it was scary. No one doubted my ability to make it work, but I did not always share that confidence. Never before had anyone trusted my judgement so often and in matters that were so important to the future of the business and this alone was sufficient motivation. Paul also shared some of the problems with me, so I was never alone in this respect. It is good to hold the reins that are long enough for a second pair of hands!

There must be something about writing in the early hours that has a greater appeal than daytime working, for Paul has also chosen this unearthly hour to sit at his desk and compose his thoughts. A wave of guilt passed over me, an emotion I had not felt since death. Whilst I had no control over my destiny, I am upset by the obvious distress that my departure has caused to so many people and I had never before considered the ramifications of death itself. I have never been one of those well known, well liked, high flying personalities that one sees from time to time, so if this number of people can mourn my passing, how much greater is the pain for those who have lost good people? A dog's bark made me look towards Paul's feet and I smiled at the Yorkshire Terrier that was trying to gain his attention. Eventually the dog won, because Paul could no longer concentrate on the job in hand. When he got up to sort out the animal, I noticed that he had written nothing. What an unenviable task!

I had forgotten about the part that animals play in our lives, but playing for a few moments with Jack had reminded Paul of my Golden Retriever. It had been upsetting when we had to have him put to sleep. Another of life's experiences that we could do without, but even the pain of that was outweighed by the joy of the fifteen years of company afforded by a truly loyal animal. He certainly gave me more exercise than I have had at any other time of my life. Paul's thoughts about Jodie reminded him of the happier times that I had experienced. To date he had been concentrating on the losses associated with my demise but now looked at the positive aspects and was able to start making some notes. He too chose a time just before daylight to discover his bed and determined to finish his notes tomorrow. Quite apart from the tribute to prepare, he had to address the problem of my replacement, something I had made a concerted effort to ignore. I imagine that the majority of us like to think that we are indispensable and even if, in reality, we know that this is not the case, there is inevitably a hole to fill, and larger in some cases than others. For some it will be an opportunity for promotion, recognition or additional responsibility but it is a distinctly odd feeling watching someone actually planning it. In reality, I have spent much of the last few years, planning where the business will be when I am no longer a part of it and have often talked about the "next decade". Many of the improvements to the premises were designed to enhance our service and keep pace with the inevitable changes that would happen, anticipating too how I wanted to influence those changes, but they are to be enjoyed in the main, by those who are responsible for the next generation. Planning for the future never worried me, and certainly that part of my brain that would not accept my own mortality was strong enough to shield me from any negative thoughts in this direction, so I have always been a part of that vision of the future. It occurs to me now of course that tomorrow's world will be designed and managed by my successors and whilst it will not necessarily be better or worse, it will certainly be different. Delegation in the smallest way has, for me, always been a hard lesson to learn, and the thought now that someone else will have his or her stamp on what I have built up over the years, could eat me away. However, in spite of that glimpse of the inevitable change, I feel no bitterness, resentment or anger. I am almost proud of the fact that there is something to build on and realise anyway that there comes a time where one is too tired to have the vision for the future that is often best left to the younger element. Perhaps my premature death will save me the embarrassment of not letting go when the time in everyone else's eyes is so obviously right. I suppose it is always better to be remembered for something worthwhile, rather than criticised for not having the nouse to realise when you are past your sell by date. As the changes occur, so the memories of my input will fade and the new staff members will not even know my name. Denise has the added burden of having to work in the same place, witnessing all of these new ideas being generated, or maybe she will decide that she has had enough and retire early from the profession that has consumed much of her life too over the years.

Denise and Bob are now enjoying their third cup of coffee and talking about the music for the service. Denise has chosen three hymns, "Nearer my God to Thee", "Just as I am" and "How great Thou art", although not necessarily in that order. Her choice is based upon the words and the fact that they are easy to sing, although she is conscious that nothing is easy to sing in these circumstances. She will be relying on the remainder of the congregation to support her during this time and hopefully, to sing too! Claire has arranged to have a compact disc player set up in the church, enabling Denise to choose something classical as entry and exit music, but she has delayed the decision on the choice of music until she meets with Brin.

Bob and Denise left Henshaw's and went home to have some lunch, satisfied that they had now done as much as they could to ensure that the funeral would be satisfactory, aware that there is a limit to the number of 'experts' that can safely get involved. They decided to leave well alone now until the day. When Brin and Denise finally met, it was as bad as it could be, and I am not sure who was comforting whom. Brin was relieved that the tributes will be done by others during the service, because he will have a hard time officiating as it is, but he has asked a colleague to help out on the day, just to be on the safe side. He discussed the order of service with Denise and then liaised with Claire to organise the printing.

Discussing the place to return to after the funeral had been a problem, and Denise was reflecting on this aspect over her lunch. I had always complained about the need to return to the house after a funeral was over, usually for a bite to eat and something to drink, before returning home. One always feels obliged to do what most people do, rather than stick to what is appropriate in the circumstances. I was always offended when listening to relatives and friends talking about the person who had died, for just a few minutes, before continuing about the new car and work and Christmas and holidays. I used to sit down and listen to everyone, gradually getting louder and louder, and I was always pleased to be leaving the house to go home, conscious of the fact that the close relatives were also relieved when the trauma was over. So I always said we should not do it. I felt that if someone had travelled a long way for the funeral, they should be looked after until they were ready to go home, but that was all that we should feel obliged to do. Now that the time has come to action it, Denise is feeling guilty about those who will not otherwise have an opportunity to speak to her and is also worried about the number of people who may be there. Neither does she feel that she can cope with having to speak to large numbers of people, when she is upset.

For years, we made decisions about the various meetings and functions we had to attend, based on whether or not we felt we ought to be there. As enjoyable as many of those occasions were, we often left home to attend them, questioning the wisdom of being somewhere we really did not want to be. In more recent times, thankfully, we asked ourselves whether or not we wanted to be there, and whether or not we could afford to be, before making a decision. As a result, we attended less, but enjoyed more, and had the added benefit of being at home together more than we would otherwise have been. I have no doubt that if Denise uses similar judgement now, there will be just a handful of close family and personal friends to look after for just a short while after my funeral.

It was while she was eating her lunch, which in itself was a step in the right direction, that Denise realised that neither the coffin nor the cost of the funeral had yet been mentioned. It is scarcely possible to mention one without the other, but it is not necessarily the elaborate coffins that dictate the cost of the funeral, although if one were trying to reduce the cost, an elaborate coffin would be out of the question. For many people, the style of the coffin is important. Whether or not it needs to be representative of the status of the deceased is another matter and was probably more important a decade ago than it is now. Nevertheless, putting cost on one side for the present, personalised coffins of today come in all sorts of materials and are decorated in such a fashion that individuality can easily be represented by the material, colour and style of coffin. Coffins can be made of anything from solid timber to

To Shed A Light

cardboard with elaborate and ornate metal furniture or no handles at all. They can be lined with satin, silk or plain domette but they do not have to have a lining either. The reasons for selecting one coffin or another are as varied as the choices available and when you add to that the do-it-yourself coffin the list is endless. There has to be a reason therefore, for deciding what is best in the circumstances but it is probably true to say that those who are going to "do their own thing", whether it be a completely different coffin to the normal one, a home made job or the funeral director's standard ready made coffin, have probably had time to think in advance about what their requirements will be and have talked about it and planned it at a time when they were not too upset to do so. Given an extensive choice when one is distraught, is not the ideal time to make a selection. In fact few people in those circumstances want to see it in advance. If you are upset and being asked to choose an item with a price tag on it, you are liable to be offended too and this can make the task of choosing the coffin, very traumatic. On the other hand, there are bound to be those who would be annoyed if the decision were made for them.

The choice is somewhat governed, however, by the decision about burial or cremation, for the materials which are deemed unsuitable for a cremation coffin as defined by the Environmental Health regulations, will rule out some of the more ornate coffins available. Whereas a solid timber coffin would have been recommended for a burial in the days before Dutch Elm disease, the conservation of timber is considered, quite rightly, to be a major consideration, and although there are still many coffins made from solid Oak and other suitable hardwoods, the veneered chipboard coffin has become more popular for many funerals.

Remembering that the coffin is also representative of the funeral director's standard, it is unlikely that you will be asked to select a coffin which is in any way, sub-standard, because it would reflect on the funeral director, rather than the bereaved, whatever cost is involved. The individual 'Moses baskets' and those made from environmentally friendly materials are seldom seen, but no doubt in the not too distant future I shall be able to look from my new environment to see them as

To Shed A Light

common place, with the traditional coffins, the rarities that the baskets once were. So what of the status of the deceased?

There comes a point at which you can no longer ignore the fact that anything other than the standard type of coffin is going to cost more, and it may or may not be a consideration. Some people will be happy to pay whatever it costs, if the purchase of that different coffin is going to satisfy their needs and it has sometimes been quite difficult trying to convince bereaved persons that the additional cost is unnecessary. For those who have saved the money especially for the funeral, the choice of coffin is very important.

My own mother's coffin was an Oak veneered chipboard coffin, and it was quite expensive at the time. As she was buried, my father may well have been tempted at the time to order a solid Oak coffin, but it was too expensive and not appropriate anyway. Despite the fact that I have done a lot of woodwork as a hobby, both furniture making (if that is not too grand a description), woodturning and carving and have always appreciated the beauty of wood, I think it would be wasted if it were made into a coffin, in these enlightened times, with all the other materials available, so I hope that Denise will opt for the veneered Oak coffin for me too. It may disintegrate much quicker in the ground than a solid Oak coffin, but I am sure that there will be no one there to see it.

In spite of her determination not to interfere any more with the arrangements, Denise was anxious to know what was happening about the coffin and she also wanted to remind Adam that she had not yet had an opportunity to see me in the chapel of rest and this was beginning to upset her. In spite of Adam's professionalism, neither he or Claire had been able to address the subject of the coffin and the cost without feeling that it would tarnish the arrangements, but Denise was not going to be upset about these arrangements because she knew the decision had to be made. They agreed a Veneered Oak coffin over the telephone and decided to discuss the costs the next day. She had appreciated their sensitivity, but that unfortunately does not pay the bills.

Having now also arranged to visit me in the chapel of rest the following day, Denise was full of trepidation. She has visited the chapel on numerous occasions, and helped many

To Shed A Light

bereaved families overcome their anxiety in exactly the same circumstances, but this was different. The thought of seeing a dead body is a problem for many people, but that thought holds no fear for Denise. She has still to accept the fact that I have died and despite all the arrangements that have been made for my funeral, all this has been done on 'automatic pilot'. It's almost like taking out a life insurance policy. I am sure that we are happy to have the security, because at the time of taking out the policy, we never expect to need it. Denise has made all these arrangements but she is still expecting me to walk through the door any moment. Seeing me in the coffin at Henshaw's will destroy that hope. She knows all of this of course for she has, as a bereavement counsellor, heard this story from her clients so often in the past but it makes no difference to the way she feels. Luke and Jane, much to my surprise, have also decided to visit the chapel and although they make it sound as if they are going for moral support I now have the ability to sense their true feelings and they are as keen to say goodbye as anyone else. They have listened to conversations about death on an almost daily basis, at meal times, or when we first get home from the office, if there is something relevant in the newspapers or on the radio, or even when we are out supposedly enjoying ourselves. If they hear of someone dying, they would want to know which funeral director was in charge of the arrangements. They would count the death notices to see if we had our 'fair share', and certainly let their friends know that as far as death is concerned, we have the answers. How different it is of course now. There are no conversations at the meal table, and I will not arrive home from the office. They are no longer interested in the obituary columns and they could not care how many funeral directors share the workload. They also realise that we did not have the answers either and they are still left with the same questions. No doubt they will be strong and supportive, all holding up their chins and discussing the way I am dressed, or how nice the coffin is, or remarking on the decor that I chose for this particular area but they will be devastated as all bereaved persons are, and they will struggle like everyone else to find a vent for their anger and frustration whilst desperately trying to remain unemotional in each other's

To Shed A Light

company, but now they are in bed, exhausted and distraught and frightened at what tomorrow might bring.

The weather was the only good thing about the arrival of the next day. The sun was shining brightly on the closed curtains and as Denise turned over, for just a split second there was no reminder of what had happened, but her pillow, still wet from the tears of her endless night brought her back to reality again. Our bedroom had been the last room to be decorated and furnished and we had probably spent longer in the planning stages with that room than any other, with samples of different wallpapers pinned up and smudges of paint here and there in an effort to try and agree the decor and ensure a good job. The result was pleasing, but as Denise looked round the room now, it afforded her little comfort. It has lost its attraction without anyone to share it, and what was our bedroom has now become just another room to clean, although even the will to do this has faded lately. Jane appeared two minutes later with a cup of tea for Denise, unheard of in the usual way, but it gave her the motivation she needed to get ready for the day ahead. As she slid out of bed, she noticed my futuristic watch on the bedside cabinet and immediately decided that I should be wearing it. So she put it in her purse so that she would not forget it, wondering as she did so why on earth she wanted me to have it now, and what use I would have for it anyway. This made her ponder about my whereabouts, not my shell, but the part of me that is telling this story. Will we be able to communicate again? In some small measure, I think we just did!

The journey to the office took longer than usual, or certainly seemed to. There was no traffic to speak of but they were all irritable, which did not help. When they arrived there was a reluctance, mainly on Jane's part, to leave the car, but she succumbed and they headed for the coffee machine once inside and helped themselves. If it was meant to be Dutch courage, it failed because by the time they were seated in the waiting room, they were quite tearful. I was wrong in my assessment of the way things would be today and about their dependence on each others strength, for once inside the chapel, they were all totally distraught and immediately went to pieces. My skin was cold to touch and that shook Denise when she was putting

To Shed A Light

the watch on my wrist. It had not occurred to her that I would still be so cold. She asked Claire, who had accompanied them to the chapel initially, if she could have a snippet of my hair, and Claire seemed quite relieved to just have an excuse to leave the chapel to do something, if only give instructions to someone else. Looking at them as I did, I knew how uncomfortable they all were with the situation. The chapel was really tastefully decorated with subtle lighting and suitable carpet. I remember going to some lengths at the time to get the nod of approval from the ladies in the office, who invariably had better taste than we men, but they approved the decoration and the furniture too! But it is not home! Whatever it is like and no matter how much time I had actually spent there myself, it was not the same as being in the comfort of our own home. As Denise had already arranged for me to be brought home, she did not pursue it any more but was pleased that she had 'broken the ice' by seeing me in these surroundings. It is amazing how much is taken for granted about someone's appearance on a daily basis. Luke thought I looked strange and distant lying there in that coffin and it upset him to see me so lifeless. Jane was just numbed and had no opinion to offer, but looked scared and pale. They did not overstay their welcome, for they had achieved what they had set out to do. They were all, in spite of their mixed feelings about my overall appearance, pleased that they had visited me there. Whether or not the coffin should remain closed in the house was something that Denise had not yet decided, but she would make up her mind when she needed to. They waited in the reception while someone went to fetch a lock of my hair, but they felt as if they were in a goldfish bowl on display. Within minutes they were on their way again, having decided that they should have had the discussion about the finances before they went into the chapel, as they certainly did not feel like talking about money now. There was no hurry for that anyway, so they returned home, none of them being in a fit state to drive, determined to try and look after each other for the rest of the day. As soon as Denise was inside the house she remembered that they had forgotten to do anything about ordering the flowers and had not the strength to go out again, so she telephoned Adam and asked him to arrange for the flower catalogue to be delivered to her so that she could choose them at home. It was much later in the day when it was pushed through the letterbox and no one saw it delivered, so they decided to browse through it after they had eaten.

Even when you know exactly what sort of tribute you want, seeing it in a brochure can be incredibly upsetting, and Denise was now beginning to wonder whether or not this feeling of utter devastation would ever end. Having been in charge of the flower department and made up many tributes over the last few years she had very strong views about what is tasteful and what is 'tacky'. The novelty tributes, like the teddy bears, golf clubs and cars should be banned in her view, and the 'gates of heaven', 'vacant chairs' and harps would also suffer a similar fate, whereas the simple sprays and garden tributes much more appropriate and tasteful, she would recommend. A single flower can express the same sentiments as the most elaborate tribute but choosing the flowers is much more complex than that. There are many reasons for sending a floral tribute and one very simple explanation is that the family has asked for flowers. These days, asking for a donation to a charity in memory of the deceased instead of sending flowers is widely encouraged and to some extent one can understand the logic to this, although I would never go as far as to say that flowers were a waste of money, a sentiment often voiced by those who favour donations. Some people, torn about what to do for the best, compromise and give others the opportunity to do either, or both. So who is likely to benefit in either case? When someone dies, one of the frustrations is the lack of opportunity to do something positive for the person who has died. Sending a donation to a charity can help, but that might be an anonymous gesture whereas a floral tribute with a hand written message can be seen and the value of the tribute acknowledged. This is often why more money is spent on a floral tribute than an individual donation. There is also some satisfaction in choosing what you believe to be an appropriate tribute, one that the person themselves would appreciate. It is important in the eyes of the bereaved to believe that the deceased would have approved of the time and effort taken to select the very best and most appropriate tribute even though they realise that the deceased is probably the only person who will not benefit from the gift. Yet there are also those who believe that a great many tributes on a funeral would be indicative of the popularity of the person who has died, so indirectly the deceased's reputation is enhanced.

As I watch Denise looking through the brochure, I am reminded of the man who many years ago was arranging the funeral for his wife. "What would you do if there were too many flowers for the hearse?" he had asked. I explained that we would provide a second hearse for the floral tributes to lead the cortege. He said that he would like me to do that, but I explained that until the day of the funeral we would not know whether or not there would be sufficient flowers to justify a second hearse.

"Fill it!" he exclaimed. "I want you to purchase enough flowers to fill the hearse", he repeated.

We spent over £2000 on flowers in order to justify the provision of the second hearse and I asked him afterwards why he had wanted me to do that. He explained that he had never bought his wife any flowers during their marriage and he felt incredibly guilty about it. This was his way of rectifying it. Who was I to judge? In contrast, if one asks for donations in lieu of flowers, there will probably be just the tribute on the coffin from the immediate family and no one will expect to see masses of flowers. It is sad to see people's expectations dashed, when, having expected many floral tributes to arrive, there is but a handful. Sensing that this may be thought of as being indicative of the popularity of the deceased, one feels obliged to find an acceptable reason for the poor show. We had a weekly newspaper in town so it was almost impossible to meet their deadline for the death notice in every case. This gave us an opportunity to suggest that people probably had not heard about the funeral in time to order their flowers, hence the poor response. In fact, it was just as likely that it would make no difference, such is the power of the grapevine, but it afforded some consolation at the time. It is true to say that for myself, I preferred flowers and although during life my hope would have been for tributes galore at my funeral, my present state will only allow me to think about the way in which the funeral arrangements generally are of benefit to my family and friends. Therefore, I can feel satisfied that

Denise is doing what she feels is right now, and although many of her decisions are based on doing what she believes to be the right thing for me, I am delighted that this gives her a sense of purpose. If it took her a little while to decide on the tribute, it took her an interminable time to write the card, or to be more precise, to think of the words she wanted to say.

When Denise visited me in the chapel, she said goodbye for the first time since my death, but the sight of my carcass was a distraction, for she was unable to see through the "shell" to the person she was now writing to on the card. Now, for the first time she had an opportunity to reflect on the warmth of our relationship, for this is what she was now relating to and the vision is of peace and tranquillity. As the tears flowed steadily down her cheeks, she wrote, "With love, as always, Denise". This was what she always wrote and it was always more than enough. Those few simple words said volumes about our precious relationship and I was 'in tune' with her once again. She reminded me now of the time we met, when sending me a card was so important. I was always staggered that, if we were only apart for a few days, there would be a card or letter on the mat, something that I never dreamt of doing and yet appreciated so much myself. She would always include a simple poem, well chosen and appropriate at the time and I would smile because no one else had ever written to me in this way before. She caught me re-reading the letters only a short while before my death, and had been surprised that I had kept them. She told me I was daft to hold on to them, but I knew she was inwardly pleased that I valued them so much. Now they are amongst those items that will eventually have to be dealt with. I wonder what she will do with them?

It took the children only moments to write the cards for the flowers that they were sharing. Unlike Denise who would always choose a blank card for her own message, they both selected pre-printed cards and just added their names. For them the important thing was the sending of the tribute but for Denise, it was the sending of the message!

The rest of the evening was spent trying to comfort those visitors who had come to console, for Denise, red eyed, tired and pale though she was, had no more tears to shed today but

To Shed A Light

her pitiful state upset those who had come to help and she ended up looking after them. She would make food for whoever wanted it, but her own needs in that direction were not being met. Only Bob seemed to acknowledge that and was quite good at getting her to eat something. He had learned a few lessons this week, and was nearly always the first to go home and suggest to all other visitors that they should follow suit in order that Denise could get some rest and for that she thanked him. She hated the lonely nights, the empty bed and the fact that I was not there to talk to and so invariably went to bed earlier than she would have done normally, but she no longer cried herself to sleep and could think sometimes of the things we shared together without getting upset. Now she was beginning to wish that the funeral could take place without her needing to be there, so scared was she of meeting all those people without having my arm to lean on, but she knew that it was not possible and that tomorrow would bring it one day closer. When Denise remembered that I was being brought home tomorrow, she cheered up and decided that she would have to get the room ready for me. She suddenly felt odd about having to prepare something for my arrival, knowing that I would not benefit from it at all, but went to sleep thinking of the fact that at least she had a reason to get out of bed tomorrow.

Chapter Seven

Although our house was not large by any stretch of the imagination, at least it had a separate dining room, kitchen and lounge. A few years ago, when I was fitter, we added a study downstairs which has been ideal, especially for Luke and Jane. I was never really sure what the room would be used for, but I have done some painting in there, Denise some embroidery, the kids are often in there with their friends and it was a comfortable addition to our home. It was appropriate therefore, that I should lie there until the day of the funeral. It was possible to use the rest of the house without the need to go into the study, so visitors who were at all unhappy about seeing me in my coffin would not be forced to do so. The study could also be kept quite cool if necessary.

Denise felt nervous and grumpy this morning. The weather was lousy and she had not slept very well, but nevertheless, she was looking forward to having me at home. Bob had found several reasons why he would not be able to visit this morning, but Denise had known that he would be unable to handle this, and had not been surprised at his obvious discomfort at the thought of a coffin in the house. It took Denise but a few minutes to prepare the room, for it was seldom untidy and there was space for the coffin in the centre of the study without the need to reorganise the furniture. When all was prepared, she relaxed a little and waited for my arrival.

I have often thought that the funeral is something that could be done 'behind the scenes' as opposed to all the other preparations and having my coffin at home prior to the funeral really emphasises that thought in my mind now. When someone dies at home, it is likely that the family have been nursing the patient for some considerable time prior to death, and yet the moment that death occurs, whatever time of day or night, the funeral director is summoned to move the body from the house to his chapel of rest. Along come two complete strangers to move the deceased and despite all the love and care afforded by the bereaved during the time of illness, their help is no longer required in caring for the person they have loved for so long, now that they have died. The moving of the deceased at this stage emphasises the finality of death and is a traumatic experience. But why do we find it so difficult to involve the close relatives in the task of looking after the person they love, until the funeral?

It is very difficult to physically move someone after death with all the dignity that is naturally expected, because of the weight involved, the difficulty with stairs and the removal equipment, sometimes the cause of death and often the difficult or embarrassing circumstances. The funeral director's staff are aware of all of these things and probably some others too, and therefore usually ask the family to wait in another room whilst the removal of the deceased is effected so that they will not be offended by the manner in which it is achieved. Those who insist on watching the person being moved are naturally concerned about the welfare of the deceased and frustrated that they are unable to help. It takes only a short time to move the patient and then the family is left to deal with the trauma of the whole experience. Saying goodbye to someone at that time is incredibly upsetting and made much more difficult with strangers present. If it were made easier for the close family to continue to look after their loved one, there would be no urgency for this farewell. The act of taking someone away from the family for what is thought to be the last time, therefore, can be worse than the funeral itself. As I died in hospital, the procedure was different but no less traumatic for my family. In a sudden death like mine, there is no nursing experience, and no last opportunity to say goodbye prior to death. In both of these deaths though, coming home again prior to the funeral can restore the opportunity to have that last time together which is so precious. For Denise now, waiting for Henshaw's to arrive, was like waiting to open a surprise birthday present with all the excitement and anticipation of a child. Yet when the moment arrived she was so scared and had no-one to turn to for help. There are many occasions throughout the grieving process where Denise would, in other circumstances, be leaning on me for support. We would in fact be a source of comfort for each other, but now there is no-one to fulfil that role and this is just one of the many holes that I have left by my premature departure. No amount of planning can prepare us for this frightening experience. Is it any wonder that many bereaved people have moments of despair? Suicidal thoughts, unheard of in the past for the individuals with seemingly everything to live for, can become a frequent consideration during the darkest hours, which sometimes seem endless. Such is the burden on our minds without a true purpose in life. So where are my relatives now when Denise needs them most? They are too helpless in their own sorrow to have any real thought for her grief. The situation is so unreal that it is difficult for them to comprehend the feelings of others. It is not that they do not care, just that they have no way of knowing the true depth of despair experienced by those who are closest to them. They will probably not want to see me now, suggesting that to remember me as I was before I died is the best solution. Due to this Denise will find herself alone with me in the study!

Once Henshaw's men had carried me into the house and the coffin had been placed on the trestles they had provided, Denise checked that everything was to her satisfaction, something she was able to do with perfect composure and professionalism. Then they left and Denise, at least for a little while, was alone with me in the house. Far from being frightened or worried, she was at peace for the first time since my death and also for the first time, angry with me for leaving her so suddenly and without any opportunity to prepare for the mess I have left her in. " Why did you not look where you were going, you stupid man?" I heard her shout. "All that time we spent nursing you through Cancer, and for what?" she continued. "How can I ever enjoy the Scillies again without you being there to enjoy it with me? she screamed. "Not to mention the kids, the house, our friends and just about anything else you can think of. How am I supposed to cope on my own?" She vent her anger for what seemed to be hours, and then her anger was mingled with sorrow and regret. She left the room, returned and left again, not knowing what emotion would surface next. She made a cup of tea, then threw it away and replaced it with a gin and tonic. Tearfully, she sneaked back into the study, full of remorse for the way she had exploded, but without any regret for the sentiments she had expressed. She now sat calmly looking at my casual appearance and smiled. "At last I have got you without a tie on!" she laughed, and knew that I would be laughing with her. We both had expensive taste in most things, but clothes especially. I had spent so much time at work or representing the Company at formal functions, that she rarely saw me during the daytime without a suit and tie, whatever the weather. Whenever I thought a casual approach was the order of the day, she would have my suit ready for me and when I was all ready to don my suit, she would ask me if I had lost my jeans. But when we gelled, we gelled, and then it was fantastic. So now she could have me dressed in anything she wanted. So there I was looking exactly as she had envisaged, and I was happy too with her choice. She sat beside me and held my hand, no longer surprised at the coldness or pallor of my skin and after a while, she did not even notice the temperature. She chatted now about the experiences we have had, and reminded me about some of the journeys we have shared. As she was reflecting on the joys of the past, she never once expressed regret about any unfulfilled ambitions. I am conscious of the many dreams that will now remain so, but I also know that once there is nothing more to look forward to, no plans for the future, then life becomes stagnant, and so I feel no bitterness either about what will never be. We had often spoken about the futility of making unrealistic plans, generally in the knowledge that they were too ambitious to reach fruition, but we were always about to win the lottery which would enable our fantasies to become reality, and so dreamt on, also aware that none of our plans were earth shattering so it did not matter if they were forever in the pipeline. As I was drifting in this world of my own, in tune with the memories that were being related to me, I was aware of the enthusiasm surrounding those stories which mattered most to Denise and they were of life's shared experiences, rather than any material gains, that excited her most, and I realise now just how valuable our relationship has been. I was listening now as she recalled with great delight the thrill of our hot air balloon ride, describing the tranquillity of the airless passage over fields in the early morning, listening to the dogs barking somewhere in the distance and watching the animals flea to the corner of the field out of earshot of the burners as we rose higher and higher above the pylons and the telegraph poles. We waved to the farmers who were no doubt relieved that it was not their field that we were to land in, and then on and on until we were ready to drift gradually down and down to land awkwardly in a cosy heap with the other two couples in the basket.

She had just finished her story as Luke and Jane arrived, bemused by the grin on their mother's face. Knowing that there was only the two of us in the house and deciding that on this occasion I could not possibly have contributed to the expression on her face, put it down to the stress of having the coffin at home, and made her a cup of tea. She no longer relied on the gin for her courage, for she was comfortable and at ease with herself. She enjoyed this cup of tea more than any other since my death and looked remarkably relaxed. Her day was spent in and out of the study without fear or trepidation and she flicked through some of her favourite photographs during the evening, shedding the odd tear, but not as distraught as she had been of late. The kids did not share her enthusiasm about seeing my body in a coffin and relied on her assurance that everything was still fine. They may look tomorrow, but they were able to go to bed that night in the knowledge that Denise had found her smile again. Denise slept for most of the night, and only realised next morning as she awoke with a headache, that she had not had a sleeping pill for the first time since my death. She had an Aspirin but stayed in bed for a while, reflecting on the day that had helped her to sleep, and almost looked forward to the new day ahead. She still had not discussed the cost of the funeral. Who cares?

There were a few loose ends to tie up and Denise actually did care about the cost of the funeral. She knew more or less what the normal cost should be but wanted confirmation so that she would be able to pay the funeral account as soon as it arrived. Waiting for the solicitor to obtain the Grant of Probate and sort out all the finances was all very well, but Denise had seen the delay and the problems that this causes and was determined to deal with the funeral account herself. She knew they would not chase her for the money and probably would not send the invoice until about a week after the funeral, but being able to plan ahead would help so she telephoned the office and arranged to call in and see Adam or Claire to finalise the rest of the details.

Denise had finally made up her mind to compromise over the reception after the funeral and had decided to ask Adam to arrange for light snacks and a cup of tea or coffee for all those attending the church service, but whilst she wanted that to be held in the church hall, she invited her really close friends and relatives back for a snack before they go home, which is where she wanted to be. Adam asked Brin if he would announce this during the service to avoid confusion.

The cost of the funeral is frequently determined by the choice of coffin and because Denise had already done this over the telephone, it should have taken only a few moments to run through the details and complete the official estimate. Denise was surprised at the generous discount that had been allowed on the professional services, due to my length of service with the company and smiled when she realised that the funeral was nearly carried out by Barklett's instead. However, she also questioned now in her own mind, as to whether or not she had been rather hasty in her choice of coffin. The reduction in the cost of the funeral now enabled her to think in terms of a more elaborate coffin and was thinking that mourners may question her judgement if only the standard coffin was used. Adam showed her through to the coffin showroom, which in fact was not as familiar to Denise as one might think. Based at a different branch where there was no display area, this new facility was still being tested, so it was easier to look at this through customer's eyes. She was not entirely comfortable with the prospect of selecting something that she never wanted anyway, and was not sure that I would want to be disturbed yet again, just for an upgraded coffin. Without doubt, the solid oak coffins with their raised lids, satin interiors and panelled sides made the plain, flat lidded veneered oak coffin look rather boring in comparison. The high gloss finish on the mahogany caskets enhanced by the elaborate bar handles, hinged lids and padded interiors were incredibly luxurious, but phenomenally expensive, and really only outshone by the metal version with its rubber seals and lockable domed lid. The pastel lid linings were adorned with heavenly designs and the deep pillows and matching eiderdowns looked almost comfortable. I suppose it was that realisation that brought Denise back down to earth and she now saw the elaborate caskets as being almost offensive. Adam had left her to browse for a while and as she looked around she saw the display area in a different light. Far from helping her to choose a different coffin, it merely confirmed her judgement over the telephone. She was saddened by the commercialism that the room introduced into what had otherwise been a sensitive approach to arranging the funeral. She knew that most people would probably be overwhelmed with the choices available, undoubtedly surprised at the vast difference in the costs involved and like Denise at this precise moment, slightly embarrassed at the thought of choosing a coffin which might be considered inferior. She knew that the customer's choice was important and that they were entitled to choose an elaborate coffin or casket that would represent the status of the person who has died, but what a time for decision making? At a time when Denise naturally wants to do the best for me, one of her last opportunities to outwardly express her affection, she is faced with this moral dilemma. She knows what she will do, because she still has an opportunity to design our memorial for the grave which will stamp her mark of individuality on the arrangements, but she is fortunate that she can think so clearly at this moment in time and is conscious of the fact that many people would select something towards the middle of the range. It was not just the sight of the coffins that upset her, for she has seen many before. In a way, she wanted to see what was available, but not like this, not displayed 'at their best' to encourage a better sale! Looking around the showroom, she noticed the other items. There was a range of dressing gowns, elaborate grave markers, floral wreaths done in tasteless plastic flowers hinting at the number of designs available and one or two stone memorials to tempt her at a later date, but even these essentials which were all available in their standard, perfectly adequate forms did not offend Denise quite so much as the cremated remains containers. The fact that I was to be buried and therefore would not need one anyway did not help her at all, for it was the subtle change

To Shed A Light

of emphasis that surprised and almost angered her. Forgetting the environment she was in and the purpose for which these items were designed, they were extremely well made and beautifully finished in a variety of materials, textures, designs and colours. Some had an inner compartment to house the cremated remains leaving an outer container for the near relative to use as a jewellery box after the burial, complete with inscription on the lid. There were some beautifully turned mahogany urns too, which I would have been proud to make, but the cost of some of these ran into hundreds of pounds and it was this that reduced Denise to tears.

This display room, originally designed as a service chapel was at present being used to test the market as far as choice is concerned. For many years as a funeral director I have suggested that there is no need to have an elaborate coffin with ornate furnishings and interior, and limited the choice on cremated remains caskets which were not expensive, in keeping with the funeral arrangements generally, but there were times when customers had asked me if there was "nothing better" to choose from. Only then would I produce a catalogue of more elaborate merchandise to satisfy their requirements and would still insist that they need not spend a lot of money in order to achieve a dignified funeral. But times are changing! Just a few months before I died, I had to make a decision about the amount of choice that should be available to the customer. It would be their choice and not my influence that decided on the style of funeral in future. Reluctantly, I had agreed to include this showroom on a trial basis, to see if the customer, left to his or her own devices, would make a better coffin selection without my influence. Commercially, it has already been a success for I see customers in the same position as Denise, when asked to select a coffin, choosing a much more elaborate coffin than they would have purchased if I had still been arranging the funeral. A few weeks prior to my death, I had been reflecting on my past within the profession and had been pleased to be nearer to retirement than to my apprenticeship, such have been the changes of the last decade. My subsequent death has enabled those more modern thinking individuals who have taken over from me, to accelerate these changes. There will no doubt be

To Shed A Light

those who are happy to spend the extra in order to exercise their right to choose what is best for them, but I feel for those who are caught in the tide and who feel too shy, embarrassed or upset to protest. The 'Claires' of the world will struggle to fit into this new regime but will be comforted by the fact that the changes at Henshaw's are not nearly so drastic as at many other establishments.

The arrangements were now all ready for the funeral tomorrow so Denise left to go back home to spend the last day with me. As she was leaving, she noticed that a funeral with a Horse-drawn hearse was about to leave the premises, so she waited to watch it go by. Neither of us was old enough to remember the days when all the funerals were carried out like this, but I had conducted a few of these in recent times. I always wondered why people wanted to spend another six or seven hundred pounds on this type of traditional hearse but still have motor limousines following behind for the mourners. Is it the show? Is it the wish to hold on to tradition in some small way or is it the love of horses? Whatever the reason, the funeral takes longer and it certainly is noticed because of the inconvenience caused to traffic going in the same direction. I was always delighted, however, that other road users had to slow down and wait for the funeral to go by. It seldom happens with a normal cortege so perhaps that is reason enough. As I watch the horses go out of Denise's range of sight I realise that I can see far more than she can now but it has only just occurred to me. My prediction for the future is no more accurate than hers, for I still lack the power to look ahead, but I can see the overall picture of the present and I can see much more clearly now, the details of the past.

There were many customs and traditions which were a part of everyday life for me as a teenager as far as funerals are concerned, which are no longer practised and I suppose seeing the horses again has reminded me of them, although they never really figured in my working career. There was bound to come a time when the memories of the past, the "good old days", would figure prominently in my mind and be compared with the present day, but I had been surprised that this could happen at so early an age. I used to smile at my father's references to the better bygone days but felt that

To Shed A Light

at the age of eighty-eight he was entitled to feel that way. It must have been the connection with a traditional profession that made me feel the same way when more than thirty years his junior.

The change in the habit of wearing black clothes as a sign of mourning has been one of the most significant changes that I have seen in the last thirty years and apart from the few that still carry out this custom, for the Italian community still do, I rarely see anyone dressed in either black tie or armbands, let alone full mourning clothes, other than the funeral director and his staff. Today, there is a feeling that as long as one attends the funeral, the colour of one's clothes is unimportant. Mourning clothes used to be an invitation to the outside world to acknowledge their grief, and friends and neighbours would share in their sorrow. A second, perhaps more subtle change, is that nowadays, the curtains at home are rarely drawn to announce the death. A decade or so ago, we would arrive at the house with the cortege on the day of the funeral and the curtains would always be closed. The neighbours too would have closed their curtains to acknowledge the occasion. I realise that more people died at home in those days, but nevertheless, there was no doubt in the minds of the milkman, baker, newspaper delivery boy, postman or casual caller as to what had happened, but it is rare these days. There was an inclination to sympathise and offer assistance, a community spirit that was genuine. The neighbours would have a street collection for flowers and the family would receive condolence cards and messages, often from a complete stranger. Now, with many of the women out at work during the day, there is no one at the garden gate to watch the funeral go by and it saddened me to walk boldly in front of the hearse almost commanding respect from the other road users who, for a brief period, would slow down, maybe even stop, while we walked the length of the street for the benefit of those who wished to pay their last respects, only to find that there was no-one waiting there. Everyone was either at work or shopping or gaily going about their business without wanting their routine to be interrupted by a funeral.

In many towns, the daily newspapers have been replaced with weekly ones, so the death notice, announcing the details of the funeral, cannot appear until after the funeral has taken place. When friends and neighbours walk on by without uttering a word of condolence, it is assumed that they do not care, but it may be that they do not even know that there has been a death in the family. So I do not consider the wearing of black clothes to be at all morbid, but merely an opportunity to invite others to do the one thing that we are not very good at these days. Talking to each other about death! Many would argue that talking about death is unnecessarily upsetting but I have seen so often in the past, the upset caused by the lack of communication. Death is upsetting and yet when we see someone in tears, we want them to "snap out of it". Some helpful crank will say, "Time heals", or "You will be able to get back to normal after the funeral is over", or some other equally distressing piece of advice and the bereaved are left in a state of bewilderment. Generally speaking, we are not in the habit of confronting the problem and yet the support we give before and during the funeral is often considered sufficient to carry the bereaved through the trauma, and somewhat miraculously "out the other side". By all means draw back the curtains after the funeral is over, but do not let those few supporters be fooled into thinking that their job is finished, for they have only just begun.

As a schoolchild I remember being made to remove my school cap and stand still when a funeral passed, to the point where I would have received a helping hand from behind if ever I forgot. This custom is still carried out by those who have grown up in that era, but they are becoming few and far between now. Men tend not to wear hats these days anyway so the custom of doffing one's hat to acknowledge the presence of a lady or of a funeral cortege is gradually dying out. If fashions change and men start to wear hats again, I doubt if the practice will return. I used to watch my Roman Catholic school friends making the sign of the cross as the funeral went by and had been impressed by their acknowledgement of the occasion and then one day, I saw an empty hearse go by and a friend still made the sign of the cross and I wondered then for whose benefit it really was. I have found a marked lack of respect for a funeral these days, but not helped by the fact that the modern funeral vehicles, being only stretched

To Shed A Light

saloons anyway, albeit expensive, are indistinguishable from most other modern vehicles from a distance. By the time one is close enough to realise that it is a funeral cortege, the damage is done, the cortege split and the offender tarred with the same brush as all the other "uncaring young layabouts" who have no regard for the dignity of the occasion. Perhaps they just do not understand? They are certainly not made aware by example now.

Certainly, because of all the preparations, now regarded as morbid, there was a greater opportunity to talk to each other, family included, about the person who had died. Having the coffin at home, almost without fail, also enabled, even forced the grieving process to start. The body was often at home from the moment of death, with the coffin being brought home at some point and often taken upstairs, with great difficulty on the part of the funeral director's staff, then called undertakers of course, to remain there until the day of the funeral. There seems to be a fear nowadays of this procedure but it did give the nearest relatives an opportunity to care for their loved one during the final preparations. "Through lounges" and high rise flats put paid to much of that, because it became too difficult or too inconvenient to carry on. Carrying the coffin out of the house on the day of the funeral, especially when it had to be manoeuvred downstairs, using leather straps and other such unsafe devises, was an absolute nightmare for the men charged with the responsibility, but the whole process involved more time and effort and consequently, a greater concentration of care for the family as a whole.

As Denise left to go home, she could not help but feel saddened at the way life goes on. She knows in a way that the hole that I have left, for most people, is like the hole left in a bowl of water when you take your hand out. You do not even see where it has been. For Denise at least, the hole is bigger and more permanent than that, and her distress is understandable. The sun was shining when she arrived home so she made a cup of tea and sat in the garden for a while. At first she was unhappy, looking around at everything that had my stamp upon it, but then she realised that the very point of it all was so that she would be able to enjoy it so she cheered up and was at the point of dozing when Luke and Jane called her. "We have been saying goodbye", they said, in a rehearsed sort of manner. "You can close the coffin whenever you want now". She knew she would close the coffin herself today, rather than wait for tomorrow, but she was not quite ready yet. She stayed in the garden a while longer, and although she had tried to read a book, was unable to concentrate so gave it up as a bad job. As evening fell and her eyes gradually became accustomed to the light, she had no desire to go indoors, but it eventually got chilly so she succumbed. She knew as she walked indoors that she could put it off no longer and went bravely into the study, once again. It was worse this time. She had known that it was not for the last time when she stood at my side yesterday, but this was different. She took a long hard look at my face, still in disbelief and held my hand for a while. She decided to close the coffin now as she could still sit with me if she wanted to, even if the lid was closed. It was heavier than she had expected and she struggled with it at first, but then succeeded and started to tighten the screws. She suddenly felt guilty now as if it were her choice to shut me away forever. She wept bitterly as she tried in vain to screw the lid down properly and had to ask for Luke's help. He managed it with comparative ease and Denise realised that this was not going to be the only time that she would need to ask for help. She was determined to ensure that people did not look to Luke to be 'the man about the house now', for so often had she seen others try to assume the role of father figure in the same circumstances. He had left the study as quickly as he had come in and Denise knew that it was no picnic for him either. Denise stayed a little while longer, but then went to make herself a nightcap and go to bed. Tomorrow is the day she has been worried about since my demise, but all the worrying in the world will do nothing to change it. In a way she was looking forward to the day when my funeral was behind her but also knew that it held no magic answers either. She had a sleeping tablet and although she tossed and turned for what seemed like hours, she eventually dropped off to sleep and did not awake again until morning. The clouds looked angry, reflecting her feelings, but I do not suppose the weather could be right for this occasion. A neighbour had agreed to sort out the food for the few that had been invited

To Shed A Light

back after the funeral, so there was little for Denise to do. In fact everyone was telling her not to worry, and that there was nothing for her to do and she eventually got the message. She looked out of the study window at the rain that was now falling heavily, and hoped it would brighten up a little. In fact by the time the cortege arrived, it was dry, although not as warm as it had been. Denise put that down to the fact that she was upset. She had been accepting flowers from florists on and off all morning and although she had always advised others that it was a distressing time when the tributes were delivered to the house, had opted to do exactly the same thing herself. Looking at the flowers was awful but not as bad as reading the messages. Jane had suggested that the messages ought to be recorded so Denise had suggested that she got on with it, hoping when all was finished that she would be able to read her handwriting. At least it occupied her mind. By the look of her eyes she had been struggling too and yet, typically, neither Luke, Jane nor Denise had talked to each other about the wretched way they were feeling. I think part of my penance must be the hurt in watching them grieve for me, unable to support them in any way.

In spite of the fact that the funeral was in the afternoon of a wet day, the cars looked remarkably clean. They had either been incredibly lucky and dodged the showers, or had stopped somewhere to leather them off en-route. They had left themselves plenty of time, but had been surprised to find the coffin already closed when they arrived. Adam had brought Ken, another colleague along to help him conduct the funeral and they and the bearers seemed to be milling about for ages in their black. Denise looked as stunning as ever in her long black dress and her wish to be strong for the sake of everyone else seemed to be working so far. Eventually the coffin was shouldered to the hearse, which in itself was no mean feat. Why do they build houses without any means of accessing the front door conveniently? Visitors had always been confused about which door to come to and it was invariably the back door that won. This was true today too, but it made the manoeuvring of the coffin much more difficult. Once the flowers and the coffin had all been dealt with, it was just a matter of dealing with the mourners. Funerals being like a

To Shed A Light

busman's holiday for Denise, she felt like organising everybody, but refrained from telling Adam what he should be doing next and everything went smoothly. He and Ken both walked from the house to the church, a distance of about two miles and probably felt like twenty-two, but it was a nice gesture. The rain started again just as they were in sight of the church, and it was that fine rain that is always determined to wet everything in sight so Adam and Ken were just a little damp by the time they made the church gate. Bob accompanied Denise, Luke and Jane, really for moral support, one of the most useful things he has done to date. Everything was ready in the church and Brin met Denise at the wicket gate. Their exchanged glances said enough and they processed into the church that was not exactly heaving with people but there were more there than I might have expected to see. Most of the seats were occupied, but the service would have been the same for two or two hundred. The music, opening prayers and the first hymn accomplished, it was Roy Crater who had drawn the short straw to speak first. In fact it was because he had known me longer than the others and it seemed appropriate that he should start. I would never have seen Roy as a public speaker. He is one of those quiet unassuming types that tend to just get on with life without any fuss, but he had obviously put a lot of thought into this tribute. As soon as he spoke I smiled and saw others too, for he was relating to some of the funnier moments of our early days together. Although he did not refer to it, I was reminded of the day when he was driving the brand new hearse out of the garage at the same time that I was reversing the van in. We met! It was my first week with the company, and so Roy accompanied me in the lift to see the boss to explain what had happened. As he was driving the new hearse, the only thing that really mattered that day, it was Roy who got the roasting and me who stuck up for him, but it was certainly my fault in the first place. Roy was well respected at the company and so the boss's wrath was short lived, it being only the spotlight that was damaged anyway, but I managed to keep out of his way for some time hence, just in case he had time to reflect on the actual accident itself. He may have realised that it was my fault! Roy was actually describing the

To Shed A Light

time when we fell asleep at lunchtime, deliberately I might add, curled up on the workbench with the coffin wadding as a pillow and a bed. How were we to know that there would be some visitors shown round? It was only three-o-clock in the afternoon. Different boss, but same temper! We both had a wonderful sense of humour and worked well together but I am not sure that the congregation will be left with such a favourable impression. At the age of seventeen in this profession, it was important to have a sense of humour. Roy did everything to try and make me laugh, usually when I was not supposed to, but we survived and I think were happier for it. The new drivers that I have employed at Henshaw's were never quite able to create the same atmosphere, although I am not sure if I would have been quite so tolerant had I found them asleep.

Roy was virtually in tears when he sat down, but he had made Denise smile through hers and they were both thankful of the hymn that followed to compose themselves. A bereavement counsellor read the reading. Jackie, who I had not realised would be there, dutifully read the words but looked at no one. When she had finished she returned to her seat and Malcolm took her place. He could only refer to the last decade, for he has known me as a Rotarian since we became founder members of the club. In fact, as a general medical practitioner, he knew me as a funeral director too, and our links in that direction caused many a laugh at the club meetings. There have been times when either because of the time involved in Rotary or the cost involved or my lack of enthusiasm at certain times, that I had thought of giving it up, but he had always been there to persuade me otherwise. How right he was, for I got to know far more people than ever I could have imagined otherwise, and been introduced to friends I would never have met. As I look in the congregation now, I see many familiar Rotarian faces, not only from my own club, but from neighbouring towns too, for in my roles as secretary, vice-president and then president, I visited all the local clubs and found them to be as friendly as our own. I remember being invited to talk to them as a funeral director and chose embalming as my subject so that I could enjoy my lunch even more. I am not sure that their lunch was as satisfying. Malcolm has always been able to get the balance about right and in spite of the fact that he sees death on a daily basis was visibly moved at times when describing the fun we have had together. Denise, sitting there listening to all of this is comforted that I have touched these lives and had a jolly good time in the process.

The second hymn, 'Just as I am', was a bit of a tear jerker and Denise found it too much although she wanted to hear it being sung by those who were strong enough to do so. The best-loved hymns usually have that effect.

David Koaley's tribute was the shortest and most difficult. He and his wife, June, are 'just' good friends but have you ever tried to talk about a friend who has just died? Part of you wants to do it because it is the last thing you can do for someone, but the major part, because of the closeness of the relationship, simply cannot. One is also conscious that there are others who could do justice to the occasion and not wishing to let them down either, makes the task doubly difficult. David spoke about the fun we had as a foursome and of the happy times spent both on their farm and in London, but what he could not speak about was the value that I put on our relationship. It meant more to me than he will ever know now, because we never spoke of it. The latter years of my life, when we saw each other most, were enriched beyond belief because of their true friendship. David and June live in an idyllic spot in the heart of the countryside, with the most fantastic views, and I have always enjoyed their company immensely.

The service continued with the inevitable prayers and to his credit, Brin has so far been able to stick to the service as it is laid down and still allow the tributes. His address came later, but Paul Mehan's tribute was next and concentrated on my working life in the last twenty years, the best in my career both from his and my viewpoint. We were lucky for each other really. I came along at a point where he needed a new manager, the existing manager having given notice to leave, and I needed someone to recognise the abilities I had. For many years, I had worked in someone else's shadow, never really having the opportunity to put my stamp on anything. I was customer driven, because there was so much within the industry that needed to change and I was champing at the bit. It was easy to make beneficial changes, because the previous manager had been content to 'plod' along, not wishing to set the earth alight nor achieve the rewards that would be offered had he done so. I was, however, more than happy to set fire to anything that enabled a better job to be done, and I was fired with the same enthusiasm that Paul was. It was his business, but I never let that dissuade me from suggesting a change for the better and he soon realised that my motives were sound. The better the job we did, the more funerals we performed and the company grew until in the last year of my career at Henshaw's, the number of funerals carried out had quadrupled during my twenty year reign. We introduced the floristry side of the business and had decided to enhance the memorial side and Denise had helped in all of that. My relationship with Paul was more than just employer and employee and after an initial period of a decade or so, I became a director of the company. I had no shares, but my ego had a boost and I felt that I was part of the family. Certainly, after twenty years, I could feel satisfied that my successor would take over a business in good stead, even if he would immediately alter it to put his stamp on the changes, although I must admit, I was looking forward to a few more years before giving anyone that opportunity. This was the theme of Paul's tribute. His appreciation of everything I did was the message he wanted to get across, but my message would be one of appreciation for the opportunity to do all that he asked of me. Sadly, no one will hear my message.

Denise's Uncle Henry spoke as a member of the family. He was good at public speaking and did not really have to try hard for it to sound well planned, but on this occasion, he struggled with the rest of them. We often have a soft spot for a particular relative, and I suppose he was our soft spot. He is a good all round handyman and always appreciated my efforts, whether it was oil painting, wood turning, carving, carpentry or general household repairs, and probably one of the best pieces of furniture I have ever made, was Alice's sewing cabinet. It is probably this that makes it difficult for him to speak about my efforts in this direction. The main point was that I used to enjoy doing anything practical and whether or not the end result was ever worth writing home about, made little difference to the amount I would turn out. Christmas, he was busy telling the congregation, was a time when they were almost bound to get something home made. I would think that they would appreciate my efforts, no matter how useless the article proved to be, and they would be wondering what shaped bowl they would get this year! It was fun for me, and it enabled me to forget about work for the time that I spent bent over my masterpiece. Denise would be smiling now, thinking of the sawdust that followed me around the house. She has certainly got many items to remember me by, but whether or not those memories will be charitable will I think depend on her mood at the time. She always said that she was allowed to keep all those items that were not good enough to give to anyone else, so she must be inundated with treasures. The humour enabled Henry to complete his mission and the congregation was well pleased with his efforts. They also understood the pressure he was under at the time.

The burial was a private affair, with most of the congregation remaining in church until after the interment had taken place. The grave was within walking distance of the church, so the coffin was carried all the way. It happened naturally, rather than a deliberate effort to keep this part of the ceremony private. They simply did not follow the immediate family out of the church until they were sure that this part was over, so the organist continued to play long after he would normally have finished. It was raining steadily as they came out of church and Denise had neither anticipated nor dressed for it. So most of them got wet, but there comes a time when even that does not seem to matter in the light of everything else that is happening. The umbrellas got in the way and were in imminent danger of blowing inside out, so they were quite quickly abandoned. When the rain stopped a few minutes later, the ground was muddy and there was no dry soil to sprinkle on the coffin during the words of committal. The sound of the dirt landing with a thud on the lid, upset Denise, for she could easily picture me lying there, and realised now that that symbolic gesture was to be followed shortly by huge shovelfuls of earth that would soon obliterate my wooden home and I would be lost forever. Those onlookers now would

To Shed A Light

not be able to distinguish between raindrops and tears and Denise took comfort from that, her strength failing her after all. It had been quite eerie, hearing the music playing faintly inside the church as my coffin was lowered into its final resting place. The members of the congregation now started to amble across to the graveside so that they could pay their respects to Denise before she left, but she wanted only to go home, now that it was all over. Today, the tomorrow she was worried about yesterday had finally happened and she was right to have had mixed feelings about the day. She could go home now and start to rebuild her life, and so to this end, the funeral has achieved something, but the rebuilding of her life would have to start with the acceptance of my death and that would be a long way off yet. I wonder if she will continue to get the support that she has had over the last few days? The few members of the family who were invited back to the house, accompanied Denise home now. She felt exhausted but at peace, and thankful that the day was drawing to a close, but was still left wondering how it could possibly be happening. After the ceremony was over, and he had dried out a little, Brin reflected on the tribute he had given, as he always did after a funeral, aware of the impact his words may have, especially on those who perhaps expect to hear more from the vicar than anyone else, in terms of reassurance.

Borin's tribute had something for everyone but the main theme of his talk was devoted not to religion, but to our Romanian trip. He did not really say a great deal, but what he said was meaningful and obviously came as a great surprise to those who did not know that we had been.

I have been drifting in my cloudy cocoon, listening to the funeral service and yet hearing very little of it, which is probably true for all those in attendance, for we all have our own vivid memories of the events which have only been touched upon during the ceremony. For me, the Romanian experience was such an important part of my life, that Brin's brief account has rekindled mixed feelings within me.

Chapter Eight

One of my biggest regrets is that Denise was unable to share the Romanian experience with me, so that whenever it cropped up in conversation, I felt uncomfortable. School as far as the children were concerned and the fact that we both worked together made it impossible for both of us to be away at that point in time, and yet I relied totally on her support, without which, there would have been no expedition. I had not long recuperated following my spell in hospital when several things all seemed to happen at once. The Romanian orphanages and the plight of the toddlers there, were reported in the media, almost daily. One of the Rotary clubs in a nearby district had recently returned from an expedition there, and their report highlighted many of the pitfalls as well as the benefits of the journey. Watching those reports and reflecting on my recent hospitalisation and subsequent recuperation, reminded me at the time, of the importance of good health compared with the pleasure which can be derived from material wealth and the sight of these naked babies in filthy establishments, without parents, proper clothing, toys, medicine, running water or just about anything else that is generally taken for granted at home, finally put things into perspective. I spent several weeks analysing the viability of such a project and eventually decided to form a group and plan the journey. The lessons learned by other groups that had visited Romania were not lost on us, and we were determined to visit an area that had not received much help. Collating the right sort of aid was also vital and the planning of the journey, the raising of the sponsorship, selecting the team, and convincing my Rotary club that it was a worthwhile project which needed their ongoing support, was difficult and time consuming. Contacting the orphanage in Negresti, our chosen village, was also complicated but vital. Delivering aid to people who had no use for it would have been futile, but the response when eventually we made contact, was favourable. Several months later, we left Huntmoor with two vans loaded to the hilt with

To Shed A Light

aid and began what was to be a unique and memorable experience for all six team members.

Sometimes, what is obvious to some, is lost on others, and it is true to say that whilst we were all a little concerned about the volume of aid we had collected in relation to the space available in the vehicles, none of us had given a thought to the weight involved or the implications of overloading them. Relief at being able to cram everything into the vans was quickly dashed when we tried to move them. I thought the power steering had failed and when I realised that it was the extra weight that was the problem, I questioned the wisdom of all our efforts. The difference it made, having decided to carry on regardless, was the speed at which we were able to travel. In the event it added four days to the trip, caused a few sleepless nights, and tested the team to the limit.

The team consisted of Borin, the vicar, Grace Pracey, a Rotarian's wife, Agnes Porato a friend of ours, Amy Sharples a member of Brin's congregation, Dick Ryan, a neighbour and good friend and yours truly. None of us had any qualifications, just a desire to be there and to make it happen, and in this we succeeded.

We overcame problems like the accommodation on the ferry, our different sleeping habits, and the language barrier at the different countries we stopped at en-route, but after only a couple of days, when it was evident that our timetable was awry, some of the team members became tired and tetchy and it was obvious that one of the first lessons to be learned was how to cope with each other. We worked hard at getting on well as a group, but we were experiencing difficulties that we had never had to cope with before. Every day brought its own mix of delight and despair. The scenery was breathtaking, the weather was at times deplorable. The roads were treacherous in parts and ideal in others. We travelled through the mountainous regions of Austria and the cold uninviting areas of Czechoslovakia, where the border guards were less than helpful. We relied heavily on our own supplies of corned beef for sustenance and were grateful for the Primus stove, even when staying at some of the hotels. Our journey through Budapest was nothing short of disastrous. Our navigational expertise was little better than our driving ability. There were

To Shed A Light

hundreds of people, as one might expect in a city, vast numbers of cars, a maze of roads, none of which led to the Tourism office, and three hundred bridges! Actually, three hundred is a slight exaggeration. It really refers to the number of times we crossed the four main bridges within the city in a vain attempt to find the wretched office that would secure our accommodation. If it were not for the five American dollar taxi ride, I think we would still be looking for it. With the team members thinking that the road we wanted was just around the corner, it was three hours later when we finally managed to find our way out of Budapest and back on the motorway heading towards Cluj. By nightfall, we were still three hours short of our scheduled stop and reluctantly, we decided to stay in Hungary for the night. The roads were unlit and dangerous in parts but eventually we stopped a lady in the street who was able to guide us in her car to a campsite. It had brick-built accommodation as opposed to tents, but there was no food or drink available. Thus we spent the night at Puspokladany campsite in accommodation that consisted of two 'bungalows'. There was one room that contained three beds together with anything else we might need. The toilet block was some fifty yards away, but at least we could wash and we had our stove and some food left. The group soon restored their sense of humour and at five minutes past five next morning we were on our way again. I think we could have started off at any time really, because none of us had much sleep, although Brin complained about being flanked by two heavy snorers for most of the night, one of the important remembrances he decided to share with the congregation during his tribute to me. I realised at this point just how different Eastern Europe was. The atmosphere seemed drab and cold even when the weather was bright. We had not heard about the poverty in Hungary so what was Romania like?

Our journey through Cluj was delayed whilst we changed some travellers cheques, the last opportunity before reaching our final destination. This inevitably was not going to be straightforward. We quickly and easily found the Bureau de Change. Can we change our cheques here? Certainly not! Only a bank can handle that sort of transaction. We found the

To Shed A Light

building easily enough. It was a dismal, old fashioned building with a grey exterior. The inside was rather uninviting too, and the two bureaucrats we met in the lobby confirmed that life was to become more complicated before it could get better. In a nutshell, they were closed. Not only were they shut, but also they were not due to open again until the next day. We explained our predicament and they took us upstairs to the "behind the scenes" section of the bank where we were greeted by a helpful lady whose English was quite good. Eventually, we persuaded them to change the cheques for us, but it was only when we handed them to her that she realised that their value was two hundred pounds. She only had sixty pounds in the bank. More telephone calls and discussions and then she agreed to take us to another bank, which was also closed but who had agreed to take over the transaction. We walked with her to another part of the town and we listened to her story about life for her in Romania. As we listened, we were conscious that her whole way of life has been so very different from our western experiences. She had been happy for years until she was able to compare her lifestyle with that of a friend in England but the pace of life is something that she would not wish to trade. I felt guilty that she was now rushing around for our benefit, but she seemed pleased to do that for us. There is much in her simple existence to be envious of too!

We passed a young girl sitting on the pavement, begging, whose head and hands were bandaged. There were no adults in sight and although I am used to seeing beggars, this sight was pathetic. Our guide was obviously unhappy with her lot but also bitterly disappointed that this was her home. Her wages were about forty pounds per week. The other bank was housed in a much more modern building and I got the impression that she was envious of the working conditions there compared with her own. Once inside they dealt with us quickly and efficiently, but I must admit, when they handed me the several thousand Lei, I was staggered by the bundle of notes. I felt embarrassed as I took the money and stuffed it into my money belt, conscious that I had to use my pockets too. As we left and headed for the nearest restaurant which she had kindly recommended, I offered her a note for her

To Shed A Light

kindness but she was obviously offended, so we thanked her and wished her well, and continued on our journey.

We were to have one more forced stop before our arrival at Negresti, because by the time we were under way again it was early afternoon and with another three hundred kilometres still to go, there was little hope of reaching the village before nightfall. By now our visit was causing quite a stir with the passers-by and the beggars. Passing through a small town called Reghin, we decided to telephone the orphanage to let them know what was happening, but this took an unbelievably long time to accomplish. Whilst we spoke about finding a hotel there for the night, we were unhappy that we had not made sufficient progress and so we battled on, determined to find accommodation as near to Negresti as possible. The route map indicated that the next major town was Toplita and I prayed that we would arrive there at a reasonable hour. It was just after nine-o clock when we drove into the town and we stopped at a police station to ask where the nearest hotel was. My "Romanian" produced the right response, and we were only ten minutes away from a hotel. I said a quiet thank you for guidance to the hotel but He certainly dished out the penance for taking the gamble! We parked outside what appeared to be a very impressive building but as we walked into the foyer we passed into a very dark and dingy reception which reminded me of an old fashioned post office because of the glazed screen between the receptionist and the guests. There was a crowd of youths gathered round a television behind the reception desk and they obviously thought we had come to join them. Ten minutes later we were given some room keys. It was very difficult to convince them that although there were three men and three ladies, we did not want three double rooms and without exception the team members questioned my ability to communicate in Romanian. In the event, we did share the facilities, if not the rooms. The rooms were on the third floor, and there was no lift. By the time I had located my room, Dick had already managed to find Agnes's room and pull down her curtains from the wall. The previous occupants had obviously died there and they had decided that the rooms must be left untouched in their memories. To summarise, there

To Shed A Light

was no hot water; in fact some of us had no water at all. None of us had water after eleven-o clock because it was turned off then to prevent the leaking pipes from continually dripping into the cracked sinks, which in turn would ruin the floor covering. I nearly wrote carpet then! Apart from being unmade, the beds lacked any linen, the toilets did not flush and the only advantage to there being no electric in the room was that we couldn't count the dead flies on the window ledge. However, that is enough detail about the best room, suffice it to say that we were not happy with the standard of accommodation. So we laughed at our predicament. We found something to smile about in everything we looked at, ignoring the décor. We fetched our sleeping bags and food and water from the vans and using the Primus stove once again, we enjoyed the last of our home made soup and cake. Agnes kindly sprayed the beds before we put our sleeping bags on top of them and we went to bed. I shut the bathroom door in the hope that I would not need to use it. I didn't! I lay in bed reflecting on the day's events and pictured the women at six o clock that morning, off to work with their scythes over their shoulders, the beggars waving to us as we drove past, the queue of sixty or more cars at the garage waiting for petrol, the ox carts, the gypsies selling Gladioli in the restaurant and the horse drawn funeral we had past earlier in the day. Not the style of funeral I was used to conducting, but the sadness and the mourning, like the respect for the deceased, just the same. These thoughts helped me to doze, but sleeping properly in those conditions was not easy for me.

In spite of that, we were all in good spirits next day, and although that hotel had been the worst as far as accommodation was concerned, it was the best as a source of fun. After that, we felt prepared for anything that might happen in Negresti. The early mist soon lifted and revealed at each new village or town, a hint of what was to come. We passed a dam, which was guarded by military personnel although the reasons for forbidding photography at this point were lost on me. We waved throughout the entire journey, to just about everyone we passed, adults and children alike. Sometimes waving both arms, the villagers were full of optimism and expectation, which was soon dashed as we continued our journey. Our aid could easily have been exhausted by now had we given to everyone who needed it, but our aim was Negresti, so we drove on. Constantly looking for shops was a little optimistic on our part but eventually we came across one that looked as if it might sell bread. The shop was small, dark and sparse in every respect with virtually nothing for sale. I was saddened by the fact that this was exactly as they said it would be but nevertheless, the lady behind the counter and another local who was talking to her seemed genuinely pleased to see us. Brin and I looked quickly around the shop to see if we could see some bread which would save me the problem of trying to remember the Romanian to ask for it. There was not a loaf in sight. We had decided to leave the shop, when I noticed a van parked outside the shop. It was full of freshly baked bread. The lady behind the counter helped me to remember the word "piine" for bread which was one of the first words I had learned and was also very difficult to pronounce but we found during our entire stay in Romania that everyone appreciated the effort made to try and communicate in their language and we were able to buy two loaves for the equivalent of our English twelve pence. When I presented the smallest Lei note I possessed, it was obvious that she would not be able to change it. So I gave her the note and told her to keep the change whereupon she gave us two boxes of matches. I left the shop feeling rather smug and also knowing that the value of the matches was unimportant. In fact I offered them to a Romanian later in the week but he just smiled and said that the matches were not worth having. I tried to light one or two without success and realised that this probably represented the quality of the Romanian products in general and highlighted one of their main problems.

    We drove on through Roman, a dirty place, and I remember being pleased that we were only passing through. Bacesti, the town that had been given much of the publicity, was not much better although it was unfair to judge with only a fleeting glance. I took note of the changes as we drove along. How different were the Carpathian Mountains of that morning compared with the plains, the dust and the dirt of the afternoon. We had stopped at Lake Bicaz to have coffee and

To Shed A Light

biscuits because we wanted to admire the scenery, but this part of Romania was not nearly so spectacular. I began to feel apprehensive as we approached a sign that told us we were only two kilometres away from our destination as I knew the scenery was not about to change dramatically and I suppose I knew already what Negresti was going to be like. Arriving was a bit of an anti-climax really. We were all relieved that we had arrived safely and tried not to think about the prospect of the return journey. We drove slowly to analyse the sort of place it was. It was quite a mixture really. In many respects it could have been taken right out of the middle of the text books that I had been reading about the country because it seemed to consist of all of those elements that were historically and politically important. Within a short distance we could see beautiful bungalows all with their own well tended gardens accessed by unmade roads lined with trees. The older people here, travelling at their own pace in their ox carts, were waving as we passed by, but not for the want of our aid. They were obviously happy in their environment and wanted for nothing that we could offer them. Just a half mile away, the story was very different with an abundance of blocks of flats which I had seen pictures of, depicting the political changes of this century. Already it was clear that Negresti had more than its fair share of devastation and change, and for us, quite a culture shock. We have blocks of flats in slum areas at home, but this was more than just a style of accommodation. The whole area was a scene of great sadness and the depravity was only a small part of the problem.

As soon as we arrived, I realised just how futile our mission was to be, in the scale of things. This was to be a learning curve for the six of us. I never doubted our motives, and what was achieved on this and subsequent visits was highly commendable but the problems of the orphanages as highlighted in the media was only one of many problems that exist and our efforts in this respect had no influence at all. We were welcomed at the Scoala Adjutatoare by those in charge, the word orphanage not being mentioned now, and their hospitality was second to none. They wanted to impress us with their efforts, and we wanted them to show us only what was lacking so that we could identify their needs with a

To Shed A Light

view to helping them. But they are a proud nation. Why would they want to demonstrate to a group of English visitors, their shortcomings as far as the orphanage was concerned? We discovered during the next few days, all that we had set out to perceive. We also realised that the basic problem was the difference between their priorities and ours. They wanted money and a greenhouse and we wanted to repair the plumbing and the windows, replace all the mattresses, inject an atmosphere of warmth and happiness amongst the children, provide them with new clothes and toys and above all, motivate the staff to help us to help them. In other words, we wanted to introduce a western culture into an eastern way of life that neither knew or cared for the luxuries of our existence. There had to be a compromise, and whilst they recognised the benefits of the suggestions we were making, they were not high on their list of priorities.

My vision for the long-term had not been just to satisfy the needs of the orphanage, but to adopt Negresti as the Romanian village that we would be able to link with at home, in order to improve their quality of life generally. This was naively optimistic but it was nevertheless and still is to some extent, a dream waiting to be fulfilled.

The one hundred and eighty children in the 'orphanage' ranged in age from five to seventeen years but as nearly all of them had their heads shaved, it was often difficult to tell male from female. The few that had been allowed to grow their hair longer were very attractive but their hands ruined by the daily task of sorting filthy potatoes. Their only possessions consisted of a tracksuit, a pair of slippers for the evening and a pair of trainers for the daytime. The trainers were issued on a daily basis by the staff, and I was never quite sure whether or not they always received their own or whether size was unimportant and they just made do with what they were given.

Our visit to the local hospital made me question our own priorities. Whilst we had brought some medicine, bandages and some useful equipment, we realised that unless you can deliver a regular supply, the idea was pointless. Starting someone on a course of anti-biotics, for instance, knowing that there was insufficient to complete the course was as bad as not having any in the first place. In fact, it may have given

To Shed A Light

a false hope to some of the patients whose needs could have been met with a regular supply of proper medication. Some of the hospital was under repair and was therefore out of action for a two-year period, and the main part of the hospital in darkness for much of the time. I was not quite sure whether it was the supply of electricity that was constantly interrupted or the need to share the available light bulbs, but either way the result was the same. The equipment was old and tatty and the whole place lacked the 'feel' of a hospital. We began meeting the patients, men first and then the women. There was a real mixture of illnesses from infected hands to terminal cancer patients with very little chance of survival, and no medicines or drugs to ease the suffering. Many of the women patients were sharing their beds with fellow patients, top to tail, and our brief chat with the more seriously ill patients was truly heart wrenching. There would be nothing we could do to help these people and our experience was worsened by their conviction that we would be able to supply the drugs they needed. I was acutely aware of the fact that if it had been this hospital that had treated me for my bowel cancer, I would have died then, as they just did not have the facilities to provide the cure. A child with a bandaged head left Grace feeling determined to return with a soft toy for her comfort, but in fact when we returned, the child had gone.

The doctor, who was also an artist, agreed to sell us some of his paintings and we hoped that the hospital would benefit from some of the money we paid. It is amazing what he was able to achieve with poor quality cardboard as opposed to expensive art paper and I am often reminded of our Romanian experience when I glance across the room and see them hanging on the wall in quality frames that would delight the doctor who painted the watercolours.

We were accommodated in two rooms at the 'orphanage', neither having toilet facilities, but we did have a wash basin with a cold water tap. If sleep had been difficult throughout our journey to Romania, it was impossible now, with so many different thoughts, some anxious, some exciting, and the little sleep we had was invariably interrupted shortly after five in the morning with the buzz of children in the dormitories nearby, and at six o' clock the yelling of the resident helpers ensured no further rest. So I got up and washed, a process that took only moments when I saw the colour of the water. It was too cold anyway for more than a lick and a promise. By seven o' clock we were in the dining room with the children. The food to be fair was as requested, exactly the same as that provided for the children, but there was far too much of it. I hated the food, which consisted of Feta cheese, Salami and dry bread, washed down with tea which also had some sort of cereal in it. I would have been happier to go without and yet the children seemed perfectly happy.

Children for the remainder of our visit surrounded us, our rooms being the only retreat, which were quite definitely out of bounds. We visited that part of the 'orphanage', used as the school and I was quite pleasantly surprised at the standard of education, but acknowledged that they had very little in terms of equipment or teaching aids. The desks were Dickensian in style and the only cupboard in the classroom contained the few 'toys' that were available for the children. Sadly, the cupboards remained locked during our visit so I was left wondering if they were ever used. There was little or no stock of paper, pens or crayons, so our educational aid that consisted of all of those items and much more besides, would be really useful. There was no gymnasium or anything to suggest that physical education formed part of the curriculum although there was a playground with a set of dilapidated goal posts. One deflated football probably meant that there were no games either. Although many of the windows were broken, something that would need to be rectified before the harsh winter period arrived, the exterior had been recently painted. They said that this was for our benefit. If this were the case, I wish they had tried to impress us by repairing the sanitation instead. In a corner of the playground were two huge piles of potatoes. The children took it in turns, in groups of four, to sort them into what was food for them and food for the animals. They then painted the pile with white emulsion to deter thieves.

Grace had brought many packets of sweets and at one point she decided to distribute them. Nothing to write home about one might think, until you see a child looking bewildered and wondering whether or not to put it in her mouth. We had to

To Shed A Light

show them how to open the little boxes to get to the sweets and how to put them into their mouths. After the initial taste, their faces altered and it was fascinating to realise how much genuine pleasure can be achieved from one small packet of sweets. The teachers were just as fascinated with the miniature chocolate bars they received and to see an adult express the same degree of satisfaction as the children, over what was to us an everyday experience, was quite humbling.

Whilst visiting Vaslui, a major town within whose jurisdiction Negresti falls, we took the opportunity to look at the shops. They too were dull and lacked lustre, were bereft of anything exciting, reminding me of a car boot sale where the best had already been sold. The goods were cheap, shoddily made, and extremely scarce. The cutlery on sale was already rusty. Leather shoes for men cost the equivalent of three pounds and gents suits were four pounds. A shirt cost one pound but the quality of the goods, even though reflected in the cost as far as we were concerned, were thought to be very expensive by the Romanians we were with. The poor quality of the paper that was used to make the books and magazines surprised me. It looked and felt like recycled paper but I am sure that it wasn't.

We spent some time with the children just before bedtime each day, and I had great fun trying to have a conversation with them in Romanian. They laughed at my inability to express myself and giggled at my frustration. We became very close because of this, and every time they met me they would mimic the expression I used when unable to find the right words to say. But they were very patient and loving and I found it difficult to move without a shadow of some sort. Throughout our stay at the orphanage, we all latched on to a child or two and would have loved to have bundled them up and taken them away with us, but of course that is not the solution. Nevertheless, it was nice to watch the team members, hand in hand with small groups of children each day. Taking the aid was satisfying in many respects, but it did not compare with being with the children, which was the main reason for our trip and what we shall remember most.

I was amazed to see steam coming from a room that so far, none of us had identified. As I got closer I realised that the children were showering with hot water. This was their one weekly opportunity to shower, most of them partly clothed in order to wash their garments too. Within ten minutes they had used all my shampoo, an obviously rare treat for them. I tried to take a photograph of these facilities but the steam foiled me. Once the staff realised that there was shampoo to hand, they joined the children, fully clothed in the shower and had a whale of a time. Within half an hour, the shower room looked like a mortuary, cold and inhospitable. They must be desperate to wash in these conditions. It all happened so quickly, that my team-mates did not even realise that they had shower facilities. As we put them to bed we noticed the dirty pyjamas and sheets and still, despite the showers, their hands and nails were ruined from the filth of the potatoes. The mattresses, which each morning were carried out by the children to dry out, are lumpy, old, torn and wreaked of ammonia.

The opportunity to sing with the children at bedtime was probably one of the things that in itself made the trip worthwhile and Brin referred to this in his tribute for he knew that none of us would ever forget this experience. The staff were not too impressed, for I am sure that they would have preferred the children to go to sleep, but Amy had brought her guitar with her and as we sat on the side of the beds, armed with a child on each leg, gradually getting damp from the mattress and I am sure at times from the child too, we sang anything that the children could easily and quickly learn to sing with us. Looking round the dormitory and watching each child sit up in turn, eager to start and wondering what would happen next was an absolute joy to watch. Some of the children were sleeping two to a bed, but whatever the reason, whether it was because they were short of beds, or whether they were brother and sister, it did not matter. It was not until we were back home that I realised that throughout our stay, not a single child had cried. They had long since learned that tears brought forth no words of comfort so tears became something they had no need for. Their eyes though, still related their feelings of the moment and I felt sure that if they had cried at all while we were there, they would have been tears of joy at bedtime when we all sang together.

To Shed A Light

One of Borin's reasons for going to Romania was to try and create a link between his church and the Orthodox Church there and this was to be accomplished within a few days of our arrival. Liviu, the priest was delighted to meet us all and proud to show us his church. It was a beautiful building in stark contrast to the tower block where Liviu lived in the heart of the town. I was naturally interested in the churchyard from a professional point of view but I left the others to take the photographs. The memorials were elaborate and on a much grander scale than would be allowed in England. Most of them had photographs of the deceased incorporated in the design but the part that fascinated me most was the inscription on each, for it included the names of those who were eventually to be buried in the grave, with only the dates of death missing. I wondered what would happen if they became divorced or for some reason were buried elsewhere but decided that divorce was not an option for Romanians.

There were no seats in the church. The congregation stands or kneels throughout the entire service. Liviu was keen to show us everything and although inside it did not bear close scrutiny, it appeared to be very elaborate. He had expressed surprise when Brin had shown him a photograph of his church because it was so plain and now seeing this I understood why. But they were all superficial. It was a very poor church really. There was a screen across the entire width of the church, also ornate, beyond which no women were allowed, so Amy, Grace and Agnes remained in the main part of the church while Liviu took the men behind the scenes. Although the bulk of the service is said from this part of the church and much of it unseen by the congregation it was the least ornate part. It reminded me of a theatrical setting where the scenery had been erected for the joy of the spectators whilst the "behind the scenes" operations continue in very basic and sparse conditions. The centre of this section housed the altar, which could be seen by the congregation through the open door, and this was very elaborate but the reverse side of the screen was drab and served no useful purpose at all. The furnishings were colourful but old and in need of repair. The carpeting throughout the church was like a patchwork quilt. There were all colours and types of carpet laid on top of each

To Shed A Light

other to provide comfort for kneeling rather than create a good impression. Neither the superficial ornamentations, nor the carpet or the drab "behind the scenes" décor, detracted from the sincerity of the priest and it was very interesting.

We left Liviu, promising to attend his service at ten-o clock the next day and went to meet the Mayor of Negresti. Valerica, our interpreter for the trip who lived locally and helped Georgetta to run the orphanage, had arranged for us to visit him and then later on, having had lunch at the orphanage, to call and visit Mr. Florentina, the Bursar of the 'normal' school. The mayor was a pleasant fellow, but having to say everything through an interpreter was hard work. He was pleased to accept two of the typewriters that we had taken along but I think that we had disturbed the television program he was watching when we arrived, because it remained on, with the sound muted, for the duration of our visit. We did however learn that he was watching a report about a coalminer's dispute which took place in Bucharest where the demonstrations had got out of hand with many people injured. Some of the patients we met in the hospital had been victims of this affray, but we were not aware of that at the time. I worried that our folks at home may have known more about the unrest than we did and may have thought that we were in the thick of it, but there had been no way of contacting them since our arrival in Negresti.

Lunch in the orphanage consisted of soup, meatballs and melons and no sooner had we finished eating than we seemed to be on our way again, this time only a short walk away to Mr. Florentina's bungalow. His welcome was fantastic. The home-made wine flowed, red, white, and black, and the food, sufficient for an army was brought outside and placed on tables under the vines. This superb hospitality was enjoyed by all. We ate and drank more than we wanted to or should have done, but they had obviously gone to a lot of trouble to prepare the meal. This barbecue had been pre-arranged and we think to celebrate the Bursar's birthday. They had even baked a cake and iced it in our honour, with the word "welcome" in English written crudely on the top as an afterthought. They showed us round their humble dwelling, which was well furnished if a little old fashioned and tarnished

To Shed A Light

at the edges. A huge wall sized mural dominated one room and looked distinctly out of place, but was their pride and joy. It was what made them happy, and they were a nice couple. The bathroom and toilet facilities were not shown to us at that point, but an opportunity to use them later revealed that the standard of cleanliness in this department is not what it should be, although better than the orphanage. Looking back as I have done often in the past, I realise that the toilet facilities throughout Romania are sub-standard but I am not sure whether it is due to lack of funds, expertise or facilities or whether it is just not a priority for them.

I joined the others outside, but within minutes it started to rain. It was quite pleasant at first. We had not experienced any rain in Romania since our arrival in Negresti and it had been rather warm. The rain was not cold though, and no one moved for cover very quickly. I have a feeling that we might have been just a little too pickled to really care whether we got wet or not and the hilarity it caused was certainly worth watching. It was good to see the team in fine fettle, whatever the reason. We had tolerated much since leaving Huntmoor and I do not regret for one second, the pleasure we got from this experience. The thunder, lightning and eventual torrential rain forced us to take cover, and the group found shelter wherever they could. I ended up sheltering in a barn with the driver and his mate who were just as merry as I was. Soon though, we decided to call it a day and retrieved Grace's notebook from the rain where it had been unnoticed all this time and left to return to the orphanage. Within an hour it had stopped raining and was warm again and we were back at the orphanage in time to sing with the children.

Although we all went to church together the next day as planned, Agnes was not happy being inside the church for long, and spent much of the time outside, although she did make an effort during parts of the service to be seen to be there. Brin was immediately ushered to the part of the church that was behind the screen to help Liviu with the service. Brin deserved to be in the limelight after all the effort he had put in and I was delighted for him. Dick, Amy, Grace and I stood close to each other in a part of the church that had been reserved especially for us. In fact one lady moved when we

To Shed A Light

arrived to make room for us. Most of the women knelt throughout the service and some of the men, but the remainder stood for the duration. Although we had been told that, as visitors, we could sit down if we wished, none of us did, but two and a half-hours later we were beginning to flag. I knew the service would be long, but not this long and Grace kept asking how much longer we were expected to stay. "Until the end", was all I could say, but after a few minutes Grace had had enough and went outside. I know how she felt and why she went out when she did, but her exit was ill timed. No sooner had she left than some members of the congregation presented us with some cut flowers. Their hospitality was touching. Some parts of the service were intriguing but for the most part I understood very little, was bored, tired and I ached a lot but this part of the proceedings added a new dimension to their normal service and we were pleased to be a part of it. Six of the orphans were amongst the congregation and had obviously been many times before. They also received money and cake from various members of the congregation. Brin had his moment too, during the service. He was asked to address the congregation, which was interpreted by Valerica who had been in and out of church like a fiddler's elbow since the service began. We were also given a lighted candle and a piece of plaited bread to hold during part of the service, the significance of which I did not fully understand but it coincided with that part of the service which was dedicated to the prayers being offered for the anniversary of someone's death. His widow was remembering him that day. We then went into the churchyard for some prayers around the grave of a lady who was preparing for her own death. That was very moving.

Father Liviu's wife was away during our visit but we were invited back to his flat after the service where his sister-in-law had prepared a meal, which included, for our benefit, fish and chips. His flat, one of Ceausescu's monstrosities was as I had expected it to be. Externally it was drab, cold and filthy and lacking in all forms of homeliness and care in an area which had been devastated. Inside, it was very pleasant, sparsely and quite simply furnished but with a warmth that was as genuine as the people who live there. We enjoyed a

To Shed A Light

wonderful evening and then made our way back to the orphanage for our night time routine with the children.

The next day was to be our last and we had one further place to visit to complete our schedule. Bacesti is a small village that contains a hospital and an orphanage that had already received a lot of attention, both from the charitable organisation that was caring for them, and from the media. This was the place that highlighted the plight of the babies and would give us an indication as to what could be achieved. They had built a play area with a climbing frame and transformed the interior of the building with kitchen equipment, renovated cots and provided clothes for the children. Sadly, when we arrived, there was little or no activity despite the improved facilities and yet within fifteen minutes the staff had dressed those youngsters who had still been in bed on our arrival. Grace, Agnes, Dick and Borin helped to motivate these children who had used the climbing frame. There were also some very sad cases and these, much younger children, were confined to their cots. The teddy bears, tied to the cots were never cuddled and these sick children needed far more help than we could give. Although it was nice to see the children playing and the transformation from being sullen to being happy and enthusiastic in such a short time during our visit, it was also obvious that our visit would serve no useful long-term benefit and I felt as if we were being shown round some sort of monument instead of having an opportunity to help. I still cannot forget the little girl who constantly rocks back and forth, banging her head on the wall every few moments but despite my pessimism, the improvements have made life more bearable for the staff and the children whose prospects are less bleak than they once were. As they get older, they will be transferred to other institutions, including Negresti.

The weather during the daytime was warm and sunny, but already the nights are drawing in and the evenings get cold. I wondered how the children would cope when the snow arrives and the remaining water pipes, such as they are, freeze and provide no water at all. Had we not been able to go back again, I would always have remembered the pleasure that was evident for the children and for us during that time and I am convinced that they will remember the singing, long after they have forgotten us.

The early start we made the following morning meant that there were few people around to see us go, but the older children who really understood that we were leaving them, were visibly moved. We exchanged names and addresses and promised to write and left in two turbo charged vehicles, and headed for home. It was only the emptiness of the vans that gave them their boost, but we had a better and faster trip home. We still waved as we went through the villages but our hearts were heavier now. It took us a little while, each with our own memories, our favourite child left behind, and our mixed feelings, before we communicated again as a team, but we slowly but surely brightened up and looked forward to going home and to making plans to visit Negresti again in the future. A group of six much wiser people left Negresti that day than had left Huntmoor just a couple of weeks before.

Chapter Nine

When Denise and the children woke up next morning, they tried to feel different, but couldn't. There were still only three people for breakfast and when the telephone rang and Denise went into the study to answer it, she was surprised to see the empty room and realised that my coffin was the item that was missing. Our friends and close relatives had all gone now and it was as if they were trying to tell her that life was now back to normal, but she no longer knew what normal was, for everything has changed. True, the curtains were now open again and the neighbours were no longer wearing black clothes. The sun was shining and the telephone did not ring as often now and it was generally for the children when it did, but there were still the few loyal supporters. Borin and Bob and Denise's work colleagues were all still supportive but she knew that there was a limit to their patience. The Cruse organisation had been an important part of both our lives and yet I had always been of the opinion that I would not want counselling for myself if ever I was in a similar position. Watching Denise moping about now makes me question that for she has always been emotionally stronger than I. Helping other people all these years and listening to the same stories over and over again have emphasised the depth of feeling for those who are bereaved but not everyone relies on counselling for their survival and in fact some are unable to cope in spite of the support they receive from several sources. Some people of course, never want to "get better", for then they will lose that support, the only opportunity for a weekly chat and a cup of coffee. For others, the loneliness is unbearable and the hour long weekly session barely scratches the surface. No sooner has the counsellor gone, than the week starts all over again. Watching the television and looking at the empty chair becomes a daily trial. No one to debate a programme with nor share the jokes. Denise and I both knew that this happened and we were helpless in our efforts to ease the pain. What could anyone say to her now, that she had not said at some point to others? Besides, she knew the entire Cruse membership, had trained with most of them and being supported by someone you know is not the same. It was as I was watching Denise searching for her sanity that made me reflect on those clients who I had counselled over the last few years; clutching for something that might help. If I were to find a morsel of comfort from the progress they have made I do not know how I could administer it to Denise, but so far I have been groping about in the dark in this respect and I have to believe that there is something I can do. Still unable to see where I am going I rely on my continuing vision and analysis of the past. It is as if I am learning, too late, from past experiences, but perhaps I have to go through this discovery in order that I might be able to help in the future? Is this to be another unfulfilled dream, or the start of my finding the right way? The first thing that strikes me is that not all bereavement has been related to death directly and many of the clients I have supported in the past have had numerous losses, which may or may not have been triggered by a death in their family.

~

For James, a redundancy was his nightmare but it re-kindled the memories of his messy divorce and all the guilt that he was living with, still unresolved, with little hope of any opportunity to do so. His wife had walked out of his life some five years ago and he had not seen her since. Even the divorce went through uncontested, so for James he likened it to a sudden death. They had no children and she wanted no material gain from any marital settlement and after a few years it was as if they had never been married. He firmly believed that he must have been at fault, but as the years went by, he even forgot why they had parted. His redundancy has given him more time at home to think about his past life, and the loss of earnings and his loss of pride are hard to bear. His losses are real, but in terms of bereavement counselling, there is no help available.

~

To Shed A Light

Maria's problem was the "baby that never was". The local hospital always referred to it as a non-viable foetus, but for her it was her baby, Jack, who had died. She was not worried about the technicalities of there not being a life and therefore no subsequent death or need to register the facts! Jack was the baby she had been looking forward to, had planned for and talked about for several months, and when she left the hospital in tears without her prodigy she had been comforted by those who had just given birth to healthy babies. She even had to return to the maternity ward and collect the paperwork relating to 'her son', but all she heard was the screaming of the newly born, and the only sight that registered was that of the tears of joy of the grandparents as they nursed their healthy babies. She was not bitter or resentful, just hurting. Her boyfriend, unable to talk about it eventually left her, with just the memories of a beautiful relationship, wrecked by nature's unfair treatment. Her scars will never heal, but those around her believe that she was strong at the time and coped well. Her daily façade enabled her to hold on to her friends but the hollow in the pit of her stomach lingers on.

~

David's son committed suicide at the age of seventeen and although there was no note of explanation left, David had been aware of some of Stuart's problems. He seemed to take his own life at a point where David thought they were succeeding in their fight against his depression. David's wife who had been killed some years earlier would have known what to do but the family as a unit had been destroyed when she died. That had been an unnecessary accident, not unlike mine really, but with Stuart being the only child of their marriage and David having to work all hours to keep afloat, it was almost inevitable that they would have more than their fair share of problems. I had been counselling David since his wife's death but the one who would really have benefited from some extra support was Stuart, but he was not convinced that he could be helped. His schoolwork suffered which just added salt to the wounds and he became withdrawn and sullen which was unlike him. When he was referred to a psychiatrist for

To Shed A Light

help, he seemed to improve but it was only a temporary arrangement and he lost the will to live soon afterwards.

~

In Tessa's case, she had worked as a nurse for many years but lifting heavy patients over a long period made it impossible for her to continue her career, but whenever there was a crisis in the family, she would always be the one they would turn to. She had been nursing their father through his illness and because she was no longer employed, was often available when her sisters were not and therefore she became his main support. Towards the end of his life at a point where the district nurses were also attending on a daily basis, he relied heavily on drugs to keep him free from pain. Due to Tessa's expertise in administering these injections to her patients in the past, it was natural that she would be asked to give the injections in the absence of the nurse, when they were required. The night before he died, the nurses were aware of the pain he was in and suggested to Tessa that if he became uncomfortable during the night, she could give him another dose. This happened about midnight and when Tessa awoke next morning she found that her father had died during the night. It was a peaceful death and no one but Tessa thought that there was anything awry, but she blamed herself for her father's death, believing that if she had not given the last injection of Morphine, her father would still be alive. In reality she accepted all the logical arguments about why she should have eased his pain and accepted to a point, that had she not done so, his death would have been far more uncomfortable than it was. She did not voice her concerns about this at the time of her father's death or even immediately after the funeral, but a few months later, she found herself in a similar position when nursing her father-in-law. This time, she was unable to administer any drugs and her relatives thought she was being unnecessarily difficult. For a while, she behaved normally, without any real signs of difficulty, but five months later she suddenly became distraught and was unable to tend her father's grave or think about him without becoming distressed. This was happening at a time when the rest of her

To Shed A Light

family were beginning to cope and they could not understand why she was so distraught. These feelings lasted far longer than Tessa could have predicted and she was surprised and upset that she, having been the strong one until then, now felt so inadequate. Her husband Roy, was getting impatient with her too, for he could see how well Tessa's sisters and even her mother were doing and found it difficult to accept that she should be feeling worse than he was, having lost his father at a similar time. Tessa could not give him a satisfactory answer and the drugs she was being administered to help her sleep and control her anxiety also prevented her from driving which became another inconvenience for the family. It took a long while and many months of counselling to deal with her feelings of guilt, but she persevered. In counselling terms, she was a text book case and I was delighted with the progress she made. I was due to see her for one last time and that was really only a formality, but before I could keep the appointment I had a telephone call to say that Tessa's eighteen year old son, Robin, had died in a tragic aerosol accident. The circumstances surrounding the deaths of her father and father-in-law had been difficult, but now they were not only having to face the reality of Robin's death, they were resigned to the fact that they may never know exactly how he died. His friend who had been working nearby at the time of the accident was not able to shed any light on the circumstances, but Roy and Tessa are convinced that there was more to the accident than they have been able to establish from any source to date. It was weeks before they could establish the cause of death, having had to wait for the results of tests taken at the time of the autopsy, and they had to wait an interminable amount of time for the inquest to take place. This was unsatisfactory too, for whilst they learned a little more, for them, it was still inconclusive. They also knew that all the explanation and analysis in the world would not bring Robin back. They still feel angry and upset about his unnecessary death and are tormented by the family occasions that he cannot share. Christmas, birthdays, his sister's wedding, the holidays that were always better because he was there, and Robin's involvement on a daily basis with the family business which was to have been his some day. They also know that

To Shed A Light

Robin was no saint and that he had probably sniffed lighter fuel before, and yet until his death, neither Tessa nor Roy had ever seen or heard any warnings about the dangers of lighter fuel. They knew about drugs and glue sniffing because they are problems which are highlighted almost daily but now they want to tell the world about the dangers of misusing lighter fuel. Certainly Robin's friends have learned this lesson the hard way but with everyone thinking that it can never happen to them, how can you get the message across and prevent any more tragedies? Roy now realises the intensity of the pain that Tessa was experiencing when her father died, and accepts that nursing his own father too, simply compounded her problems. Now they are united in their grief, but having shared the same feelings so often without finding any solutions, consolation or comfort, they do not know what else to say to each other about Robin. They have gone over the same ground so often, that it all seems pointless now. Some of Robin's distant friends and relatives requested a photograph of him, something that Roy could not bare to deal with. Tessa found a suitable negative and a local photographer produced some fine prints which Tessa has now distributed, but it took a great deal of courage to sort them out and post them off. Robin's girlfriend, Janice, has been a source of tremendous comfort to Roy and Tessa, both before the funeral and afterwards, but now every time Tessa sees her, she is reminded that Robin is no longer around and partly resents her continuing visits. She is sure that one day, Janice will have a new boyfriend and she does not know how she will cope with that and feels that it would better if her visits were curtailed. The other part of her is appreciative of all that Janice is doing and she feels guilty about the depth of her selfishness. I was visiting them until recently, knowing that they will never get over his death. The deaths of Tessa's father and father-in-law have paled into insignificance in comparison with this tragedy. I do not think I have ever seen a family so distraught.

~

Suddenly, in all of these thoughts, the memories of my own mother's death were more vivid than usual and I reflected on

To Shed A Light

the implications of her illness and death within my family. Elaine and I were just seventeen years old when she died, and Garth and Kevin just a few years older. She had been ill, if my memory serves me correctly, for at least three years prior to that. Many of the operations that she underwent during that time are commonplace today and not nearly as serious as they were thirty years ago. Even the Radiotherapy treatment, always regarded as a last resort in those days, has saved the lives of many others since. The things I want to forget are often uppermost in my mind. The bus journey to the hospital to visit her was a chore and I hated visiting time. We used to chatter about all manner of things to start with, but the last half-hour dragged. The ward was too warm and impersonal and I had no idea how ill she was. It is only now with hindsight that I wish I could have those days back again to say the things that have been left unsaid. I feel guilty that I complained about the journey to the hospital. How I wish I could visit her now! She has been unable to share in my happiness or advise me when things went wrong and our family unit was affected by her leaving so prematurely. When I think now about the influence she has had on my life, in spite of the fact that she has not been here to share it, I understand more fully the need to remember her, rather than try to forget. As painful as it can be sometimes, in order to relate to the good times, I have first to overcome the barrier of the sick bed downstairs, the hospital visits, the anguish on her face, without fully understanding why, her coffined body and the funeral, before I can picture her as she was before she was ill, when she was the doting, caring mother we had all come to love and respect. I can see those days more clearly now but it has taken years of counselling others, to realise that what is true for them, has also been true for me over the years.

~

Mr. Hardy, for I never knew his Christian name, had an experience that we talked about for just an hour. He wanted to voice it, but did not want a regular visit. At sixty-five years of age, and only recently retired, with everything to look forward to, his wife, Joan, became ill and died within a month

To Shed A Light

of diagnosis. He was and still is a keen golfer, and has a few friends who regularly play golf with him. When Joan died and the funeral was over, it was within a fortnight that they asked him for a game, and although he did not feel up to it, he was also aware that he needed his friends, so agreed to play. Throughout the match he was constantly talking about her and they were keen to listen which gave him the heart to play again the following week. Within minutes of starting their game, Mr. Hardy felt uncomfortable, for he sensed an awkwardness whenever he mentioned Joan's name that had not been apparent at their last meeting and so felt that he should not mention her quite so often. The third time they played he knew that he could not mention her name at all, for they had become bored with the conversation and probably embarrassed too. He still plays golf, but they never speak about Joan now. They, in turn, think that he has got over her death, as he no longer mentions her name.

~

Christine's story is a very special one. In her I see a great many problems that are experienced in one way or another by so many bereaved people. Her husband, Patrick, died over a decade ago when they were living in the London area and in order to comprehend the total devastation that his death caused, we have to picture her lifestyle before Patrick became ill, relate to the trauma of nursing him until he died, describe the arrangements which were made for his funeral and understand the many changes that have taken place in her life since.

Christine met Patrick when being interviewed for a job in Commercial Television and they started working together in a venture that in those days, over forty years ago, was quite a gamble. They worked hard and played hard, sharing everything and immediately formed a wonderful relationship. As Commercial Television gradually took off, so did their lifestyle. Travelling for the business took them all over the world, then there were holidays abroad and an amazing social life including parties and the making of new friends. They supported each other over many years and enjoyed their house

To Shed A Light

and garden, the nightlife, the expensive cars, a yacht and the excitement usually only fulfilled in dreams.

It was twenty-eight years later, then running their own business, when Patrick started to feel very tired all the time. He was diagnosed as having Cancer and immediately had an operation to remove a lung. At this point there was no question of it being terminal and the doctors assurance that all would be well encouraged them to support each other and find that determination to beat it. Christine, during this time, was managing the business and the home, whilst trying to nurse Patrick back to full strength, sometimes in hospital, often at home. The business started to founder and just over a year later, Patrick became ill again. A short while afterwards he was given only six months to live and they needed all their strength to cope with their new situation. They decided to sell their house and move into a flat nearer the hospital. Conscious perhaps of the trauma they were experiencing, it was suggested that they should meet with a Macmillan nurse, but her advise consisted of having to "come to terms" with the problem which upset them even more. They wanted information about how Patrick would die, whether there was anything they could do to make him more comfortable and what treatment he would be getting, but they could never get an answer. Christine was left feeling bewildered and betrayed, having been given the surgeon's promise that he was completely cured, and now just twelve months later, they found themselves facing the inevitable again. Installed in a leased flat a short distance from the hospital, having now sold the house, Patrick suffered various side effects to his treatment and started to get weaker. He lost his appetite and needed more help and specialist treatment that would see him in and out of hospital for days at a time. During this period, they talked to each other about how she would cope after his death and Christine felt reassured, due to his confidence in her. Patrick was also comforted by the fact that she was so strong. As the months passed by, the lease was running out on the flat so they decided to purchase one in the adjacent block. The formalities were being finalised, and arrangements made for some repairs to be carried out, for the new flat had been neglected and needed quite a lot of

To Shed A Light

work doing to it, when Patrick developed a chest infection and within hours he was back in hospital again. Later that same afternoon, he was laughing and joking with an old friend who had visited him and Christine was pleased with the progress he was making. They had often spoken about the way it would be for Patrick when he died, and the only real promise that Christine could make, was that she would be with him even if she could not ease his pain. That night, Patrick asked her if she would stay the night, but Christine was worried because she had arranged for the plumbers to install a new central heating system and bathroom first thing next morning in the new flat and wanted to ensure that all was ready in time for his discharge from hospital. She stayed with him until eleven o-clock until he was sound asleep and then consulted the doctors. They assured her that there would be no problem if she went home and they would contact her if there were any change. She therefore decided to go home and return as soon as she had organised the workmen. She arrived home about forty minutes later and decided to telephone the hospital before going to bed. The nurse who answered the telephone to her said that Patrick had died five minutes after she had left the hospital.

In a blind panic she telephoned her sister, but was almost too distraught to speak.

"I shouldn't go to see him if I were you", her sister advised. "I should try to remember him as he was before he became ill. There's no need to put yourself through that trauma." Christine accepted her advice and decided to return to the hospital the next morning to deal with his belongings. She had no one else to talk to and at that time of night, thought that she must not disturb anyone. She sobbed bitterly for hours asking herself constantly why she hadn't stayed at his bedside as she had promised she would. Why had the doctors not been honest with her? They must have known that he was close to death. She had numerous questions and none of the answers but she was racked with guilt about her own failure. All she had to do was to be there! Now she wanted to know if he had woken up before he died, or whether he was aware of the fact that she had slipped out while he was asleep. Perhaps he had waited for her to go. She wondered what the doctor was doing that was so important that he could not find the time to tell her what was happening, and what about the nurses? Surely someone cared about him. Her emotions changed from anger and resentment, to fear and self-pity and then to disbelief and sheer numbness. Exhausted, she lay down on the settee, too frightened to go to the bedroom and not wishing to look at his half of the bed. She was unable to sleep or concentrate on anything during that endless night and was still awake when dawn broke.

The sound of the rain hitting the window alerted her to the fact that this first dreadful night was over and she tried to gather her thoughts from the previous day, but could not believe that it had really happened. In her sorrow, she had forgotten that the plumbers were coming and was startled when they rapped on the door. She knew the work had to be done and decided not to tell them about Patrick. Instead she made certain they were able to cope in her absence and got ready to go to the hospital. She had only been in the flat a matter of days and knew no one in this block. Looking an absolute wreck and not caring about her appearance either, she left the flat and wandered aimlessly around for an hour or so, not really knowing what to do and yet being aware of the need to take control of herself. Eventually she found herself walking in the direction of the hospital, which was a futile exercise as it was much too far to walk. She returned to get her car and got soaked in the process but ignoring her appearance and discomfort she carried on to the hospital, assuming that she would be able to park her car in one of those specially reserved places. The car park attendant pointed her towards the general parking area, knowing full well that it would be nigh on impossible to find a space. If he wondered how someone could get so wet when driving a car, he never said. Christine had decided in her own mind that everyone by now would know about her plight, but from their reaction so far, they obviously didn't. She was not feeling strong enough to argue, and headed for the car park. She abandoned her car in a space that was not really designed as a parking spot but she was too tired and upset to think of making a better job of it. "Can we help you?" she heard the receptionist ask but her voice was in the distance and she ignored her and made her way up to the ward, detesting every step of the way. She looked at the dreary walls of the corridor and the staff busying themselves with their daily routine unaffected by her trauma and that offended her too. The one nurse she had trusted to look after Patrick, and who had not been on duty when he died, had not been informed either, so she was not only shocked when Christine told her what had happened, but was visibly moved. Watching her walk away in tears somehow gave Christine a new sense of purpose. Somebody does care after all, she thought to herself. She was not going to get a satisfactory answer from the doctors today, so concentrated her efforts on those practicalities that the patients' affairs officer had clinically told her about. She collected the death certificate from the ward sister who was obviously embarrassed, picked up his clothes which had already been parcelled up for her, and left the hospital to go home. She was neither into one flat nor out of the other and so went to the leased flat because Patrick had shared that with her. They really had not been there long enough for it to be home in the true sense of the word, but Patrick's last few months there had been happy ones, when he had been free from pain. She sat in the armchair, the one that was Patrick's. The one she had decided not to take to the new flat. From that position she could see all that Patrick had seen from the large picture window, overlooking the estate. Concorde had flown over daily and he never once failed to mention it. Although he had been to America many times before, he had only been in Concorde in his dreams although that had been quite often lately. Christine was aware of the fact that she now had something in common with the pilot. She too was operating on automatic pilot. There was no other explanation as to why she had suddenly decided to go to the hospital and deal with his belongings. She picked up the Yellow Pages and thumbed through the section on funeral directors. She could have used a pin to find one, for she knew none of those listed. She telephoned Frank Jennings & Sons, partly because she liked the style of the advertisement but also they were nearby. He volunteered to come to the flat to see her about the funeral arrangements and within an hour or two, she was giving him instructions. It could have been a solicitor talking to a bank manager, so clinical was the interview. She had her questions answered, but not having arranged or even attended a funeral before she did not know what to ask and there was very little in the way of volunteered helpful information. It was to be a cremation. She and Patrick had discussed the funeral arrangements and had talked about cremation, but it had not been the right time to analyse or compare what alternatives there were and Patrick at the time, being full of confidence, was convinced that Christine would cope better too if she did not have to go through the anguish of watching his coffin being lowered into a grave. This was a conscious decision, but also based on the fact that seventy per cent of the population opt for cremation these days, so it must be the best. His ashes were to be scattered in the Garden of Remembrance at the crematorium for similar reasons. No mention was made of the chapel of rest, nor starting the funeral from his home. The idea that they should meet at the crematorium using their own cars just cropped up in conversation as they spoke generally. These arrangements too, were being made on automatic pilot. There was to be no clergyman at the crematorium because neither Christine nor Patrick was very religious. Within half an hour the funeral had been arranged and Christine was left to reflect on the details that had been organised. She saw no problem with what had been arranged, and she was convinced because of Patrick's confidence in her, that she would cope well when everything was over. The funeral took place a few days later and bit by bit she moved all her possessions into the new flat. With the exception of a trunk which contained a large number of photographs and some other personal possessions, mostly belonging to Patrick, which Christine took with her, it was convenient to dispose of Patrick's clothing and the other unwanted personal items, rather than move them all to the new flat and then sort them out there. She telephoned the Salvation Army who collected the useful items of clothing and determined to make a fresh start in the new flat, disposed of many items of furniture that might bring back any unwanted memories, replacing them where necessary with new furniture. So life in her new home, which was originally to be their home, started almost from day one without anything to

To Shed A Light

remind her of Patrick. The trunk containing the photographs, too painful to deal with, remained unopened. There was a great deal to do in terms of decorating and repairing so a lot of Christine's time was spent sorting the flat out. She gradually became acquainted with her new neighbours, who knew that she was a widow, but did not see any reason to broach the subject and Christine never did. Life was for a few years, lived "normally". During the latter part of Patrick's life, when he was so dependent on her, she was coping on all fronts, so to continue was easy. In fact, she had more time on her hands now that she was no longer having to nurse Patrick. The business, however, had now folded leaving her with the time-consuming problem of helping to wind up the Company affairs. There was little or nothing left to salvage from the business and she no longer enjoyed the wealth or the lifestyle of their previous existence. Her "friends" were only around as long as the champagne was flowing and by now she had lost touch with all but one or two. Perhaps it was because of her busy life of recent years which had made it difficult to maintain the contact with her family that she would have liked to, which now meant that she saw very little of them. They spoke on the telephone quite regularly, but after a while it was seldom about Patrick. Christine always tried to put on a brave face and give her family the impression that she was coping reasonably well so they generally referred to the life that she was living at that time, rather than the life she had shared with Patrick. Christine, being an easily motivated person with an enthusiasm for challenges generally, was asked by her neighbours to join the local Residents Association and she readily agreed. For a couple of years she chaired the meetings and achieved a great deal, but the cost of living in her London flat, the fact that she was so far away from her family and the lost friendships of the past made it impossible to stay. So she sold her flat and moved to be closer to her family. By the time she had paid the legal fees and moving expenses she could afford to buy only a modest Council house and as Christine was unfamiliar with the area she had no way of knowing just how bad the area was. Tenants that have been re-housed for one reason or another occupy ninety per cent of the accommodation and the area has deteriorated badly.

To Shed A Light

Christine had sufficient money for carpets, curtains and eventually, double-glazing. There was a small enclosed garden that had been badly neglected, like the neighbouring gardens, but there was scope for her plans. Charlie the cat, who had kept her company and probably saved her sanity over the last few years, accompanied her to her new home and together they settled down well. The neighbours, albeit from a different background, seemed genuine and friendly and for a few weeks at least, Christine was able to adjust to her new surroundings.

It was inevitable that eventually she would take stock of her situation, comparing her life now with the way it had been with Patrick. Whether it was the complete change of surroundings, the closer proximity of her family, her own failing health, an acceptance of the reality of Patrick's death or a combination of all those things, is difficult to tell, but within a few weeks of sorting her new home out she woke up one morning in as distraught a state as she had ever been, apparently without good reason. She was confused about her state of depression but was not really surprised about the intensity of her feelings for Patrick. There had been numerous days during the last decade where her survival had depended on her ability to refuse to accept what had really happened and although part of her knew perfectly well that Patrick was not about to walk through the door, she was determined not to acknowledge it. The battle within her had been raging since the day he died but on this particular morning she was unable to exercise the control that had kept her going all these years. Even now, her analysis of the way she felt centred on the fact that she had been in considerable pain recently, and it is true to say that this was certainly a trigger. Her neighbour happened to call round to borrow some sugar, which was not very original but it was the excuse he used to pop round and say "Hello!" She was so embarrassed that she tried to send him packing but he insisted on staying until she was composed again. She had perfected the knack of composing herself quickly for the benefit of others and soon she had convinced her neighbour that it was just the relief of getting her home sorted out and that she would be fine from then on. He was satisfied, and left her with her own thoughts for the rest of

To Shed A Light

the day, promising to call in the next day just to confirm that she was still alright.

As soon as he left, she burst into tears again, but this time she was angry with herself for allowing a virtual stranger to see her in that state. Nevertheless, she was also worried about the way she was behaving and sought an explanation from within.

She did not have to look far, for these feelings were not new to her. Only the way she expressed them and the timing surprised her.

For quite some years, long before Patrick became ill, she knew that she was having problems with her hip. It was only uncomfortable to start with and she dismissed it at the time. When the discomfort turned to pain she decided that she would have to consult her doctor who in turn referred her to an Orthopaedic surgeon. It was confirmed that eventually, she would need a hip replacement but they agreed that it should be put off until it was absolutely necessary, mainly due to her age. Now the pain was becoming unbearable and she knew that she could delay the operation no longer. She had also suffered from Migraine on a fairly regular basis over many years and those bouts of headache seemed to be more frequent lately. The noise in her ears, not yet diagnosed as Tinatus, added to her distress and all of these things gave her a satisfactory explanation as to the way she was feeling that morning. It was on a routine visit to her doctor to discuss the possibility of a hip operation, that the locum who happened to be standing in for her own doctor, asked, "Have you had a bereavement recently?" She was flabbergasted and the fact that he was not surprised when she told him how long ago it had been, made matters even worse. To cap it all, he suggested that she made contact with Cruse, the bereavement counselling organisation, because he felt that she badly needed support. All this was an aside to the appointment he made for her to see the surgeon again regarding her hip operation, but she went home questioning his sanity.

It was just one hour later when she decided to take the doctor's advice, but it was to be two weeks before a counsellor would be able to call, during which time, she reflected on her life since Patrick's admission into hospital for the last time.

To Shed A Light

Time had mellowed her anger at the lack of information regarding Patrick's treatment and prognosis but she would never forgive them for putting her into a position where she would break her promise to Patrick. He had never asked her to stay with him before and she thought now with hindsight, that he must have known that he was dying. No-one can tell her now whether he died peacefully in his sleep, knowing that she was by his side, or whether he had woken up to find her gone. If he died so soon after she had left his side was no-one able to judge how close to death he was, and thus advise her to stay awhile? Christine knows all the reasons why she was right to do what she did at the time, that her actions were based on the information she was given, and that anyone in the same position would have acted in the same way, but it does not help. Had she had another opportunity to see Patrick, either at the hospital after he had died, or at the Chapel of Rest at Frank Jennings', she may have felt less guilty, but in her distraught state at the time of death she was vulnerable and accepted the advice of those who should have known better but did not understand her situation. Some people can cope with seeing their near relatives after death whilst others do so out of a sense of duty. The next patient may well have needed Patrick's bed and the hospital mortuary may not have been the ideal environment in which to see him, but someone could have told her that she could see him at the funeral home. His sudden death, for that is what it was in her eyes, had cheated her out of the opportunity to say goodbye despite the fact that she knew he was dying. She could not hold his hand or stroke his forehead or have the conversation with him that she feels is so important now and in all the years since his death, she has never been able to forgive herself for that. She forgot to ask for a lock of hair and she had no idea what clothes he was dressed in. Perhaps she should have provided some? The strangers that 'looked after him' would have known nothing about him. At the time it did not seem to matter, if indeed it even occurred to her, but now, with all the regrets that she has about what happened, it certainly is important. It may be that there was someone looking after him who really cared, but she would never know now and it was so important at the time to think that he was being treated like the special person he was. In spite of the fact that they had talked about his death, she realises now that she had never really grasped the reality of what was happening, hence her distraught state immediately afterwards and her inability to communicate effectively to the funeral director any of her wishes regarding the funeral. Christine can remember very little of what happened at the time, and she was so totally confused anyway, she had not been prepared for the questions so how could she be certain about the answers? She is certain now! She may be nearer to her family but she is even further away from Patrick, not that she has visited the crematorium in the last decade anyway. What on earth is the point of going back to a building that holds only the memories of the worst day of her life, or to be more accurate the day that started the worst period in her existence? Besides, talking to a page in the Book of Remembrance hardly compensated for the missed opportunity to speak to Patrick.

Christine was amazed at how angry she was getting. After all this time, she felt as if it was yesterday and her frustration and distress was as acute as ever. She wondered why she had made some of the decisions that now she regrets so much. Nothing has changed, so if the decisions are right now, they must have been logical at the time and yet she succumbed so easily to the suggestions that were put to her then. She and Patrick had spoken about the idea of burial or cremation, but they were more concerned about his welfare and her ability to cope in his absence, rather than the practicalities of disposing of his body. There may be a right time to discuss that, she thought, but it was not when people were healthy as the subject never arose, and it would be wrong to broach the subject when the person was ill. When they are dead it is too late. Without doubt, she regretted their decision to opt for cremation and now she thought that seventy per cent of the population must be asked to make a decision whilst they were too distressed to analyse the subject, if the statistics were to be believed. Actually, the decision to have Patrick cremated was easy. The difficult and much more painful decision, the one that she was now regretting more than anything else, was what she had done with his cremated remains. She has learned from just about everyone she speaks

To Shed A Light

to on the subject now, not that there are many, about the various options that are available these days, and scattering the remains at the crematorium is quite low down on the list. She could have kept him at home, buried his remains in his parents' grave, interred them in the local churchyard, buried them at sea, taken them to a Woodland burial site or numerous other options which would have given her a spot to visit. But at the time she knew nothing of those options.

There had been an 'open day' at her local crematorium many years ago, and to please a friend she had accompanied her on the visit. Prior to that she had been convinced that you would not get the correct ashes back, that they probably used the coffins more than once, or the handles at the very least, and that the jewellery would be sold to the highest bidder. Having seen the methods used to pulverise the bones after the cremation, in order to achieve the cremated remains, she felt comfortable about this aspect. At least she knew that Patrick's remains had been dealt with in accordance with her wishes, even if with hindsight she could think of something more appropriate for him. She had always thought that the handles were brass too, as opposed to the environmentally friendly plastic that was used so she understood why no-one troubled to remove them. It was stupid to believe that the coffins were re-used as well, but it had made for a good story at the time. The jewellery was the only thing she nearly got angry about again, but then she remembered that this was the one thing she was adamant about. His ring had to be removed. She realised at this point that she had been asked for her instructions about his jewellery and may well have been given other options too, but she may have been too upset or angry to take it all in at the time. In the same way that the 'ceremony' had happened around her, whilst her thoughts had been anywhere but there, it is quite possible that she had heard only a fraction of what she was being told. She remembered thinking after the service, when all her friends were saying how fitting it had been, and how appropriate it was that she had heard very little of it.

As her thoughts went back to the funeral, she remembered being given a booklet by the funeral director, which explained his services, so, not really knowing why, she decided to recover it from the trunk and read it now. She had put the trunk upstairs in her bedroom, and frequently gave it a sideways glance as she got into bed, but she had never been able to pluck up the courage to open it. Today, for different reasons, she would open it and bypass the photographs to retrieve this booklet, which for some reason now, seemed important. As soon as she got to the door of her bedroom she knew that she would be unable to open the trunk. This was going to take far more courage than she could muster today and in fact suddenly felt guilty about what had happened to all his other possessions. She had an overwhelming desire to visit Patrick, wherever he was at that moment, but realised, not for the first time, that there was nowhere to go. She wondered why she had missed out on anything tangible but most of all, she realised just how final cremation was, and that was the upsetting aspect for her. If only she could visit a spot and talk to him now but she is left with the memories and they are too painful to contemplate. The funeral arrangements had been bad enough, but as she thought of her life since then she realised what a sham it has been. Never once has a day gone by where Patrick hasn't figured in her thoughts or actions in one way or another and yet to the outside world she was a woman coping with daily life as any other. Neither had she been aware of this reliance on his invisible support, constantly seeking his approval for the decisions she made, sharing her life with him but receiving nothing in return other than the comfort of knowing that even death could not separate her from his love. At the height of their careers, when everything was magical, economising would mean having only one bottle of wine with their meal instead of two whereas now, a far cry from those days, it meant wearing a cardigan to keep warm instead of having the heating on. Christine has always been sensible about the need to eat and keep warm and with the help of Social Security she was now always able to achieve that, but how she longed to return to the Cotswolds for a short holiday or spend some money on plants for her garden without having to juggle the funds to do it. Finding the fuel for her car so that she could visit her family was a major achievement, and yet there were others far worse off than she was. She was surrounded in fact, by people who had never

To Shed A Light

been on holiday and Christine kept reminding herself of this perspective. Her painful hip made it extremely difficult to move about comfortably, and she would often lie on the floor to try and ease the pain. Gardening, her favourite pastime, was getting almost impossible to do now and this was one of the reasons that made Christine's mind up about the operation.

It was about this time that she contacted Cruse. On my first visit, she had given me the date of her operation so our counselling sessions were a bit disjointed at first. A few weeks later she was recovering from the operation but it was not really a success. Either her expectations were too high or the doctors were optimistic about the benefits because with the possible exception of a week or two, she has never been pain-free since. Sometimes it hurts more than it used to prior to the operation and she has often said that she regretted having it done.

With so many other bereavements in her life, including her loss of mobility, it is not surprising that her progress was slow. Without Patrick by her side she had no desire to join any local clubs but regretted sometimes not having a religious faith, because she felt that there would be more scope for getting to know people and mixing with members of the community if she attended a church or similar organisation. She was not active enough to work and yet in this respect she had a lot to offer. What she could have earned in wages from a part-time job, even if her health had allowed it, would have been deducted from her benefits anyway, so she stayed at home. She had very few friends, and those that she had, she hardly saw, because of the distances involved, and yet she would still make great efforts to 'entertain' them on the rare occasion when they visited her. It would then take weeks of lowly living to rebalance the budget, but her friends would not realise that.

One morning, having woken up early to see the sun trying to make an entrance through the closed curtains, she decided to get up and draw them, for she loved the sunshine at this time in the day when it was not too hot. But as she was getting out of her bed, she moved awkwardly and lost her balance. She put out her arms to save herself but all she could grab

To Shed A Light

hold of to break her fall, was the trunk, which toppled over in her effort to use it as a support. As it fell over, the lid opened and everything spilled onto the floor. Miraculously, she was not hurt, but the shock of ending up in a heap on the floor was only slightly less horrific than seeing all the photographs strewn over the carpet. She sat there in a daze for some minutes, trying to compose herself. She knew she should be crying now, because that is what usually happened at a time like this, but a photograph had caught her eye. She picked it up off the floor and smiled. This was a photograph of Patrick as a young man and she had forgotten that she still had it. It must have been taken about a year before they had met, because she remembered the suit he was wearing. She could have just bundled them all back into the trunk, but she knew now that she would start to put them into some kind of order. Some brought tears, others she was unhappy about but she even laughed out loud at one point. By the time she had replaced them in the trunk, having looked at all of them, she was beginning to feel stiff from the position she was in. When she looked at the clock it was nearly midday. It had taken her over four hours to sort them out, but more importantly, she could not believe that she had been able to look at them.

Her favourite photograph of Patrick was on a snapshot of the pair of them, taken at a dinner dance some years ago. She was not too happy with her own expression, but she decided to take it to the photographers to see if she could get it framed. The next day, having recovered sufficiently from her fall, she achieved her aim and a week later it was hanging on the wall for all to see.

That was really the turning point for Christine. Her life will never be back to "normal" as expected by the outside world for that would have to include Patrick's return but she is able to look at his photograph and talk to him as she used to without becoming distraught and that in itself is a major step forward. She has promised to show me the rest of the photographs...one day!

Chapter Ten

A few months had elapsed since my funeral and Denise, Luke and Jane were getting on with their lives as best they could. They were in regular contact with my sister and my father and spoke to other members of my family with whom we had not been in touch for years, but it was always hard to talk over the telephone. One morning, Bob telephoned to see if he could call round to see Denise, which in itself was unusual, because he normally just appeared, uninvited. Denise decided that there must be something specific he wanted to talk about. He had been there about half an hour, and was part way through his second coffee, when he was obviously struggling to find the courage to broach the subject. Denise helped him out.

"So 'spit it out', Bob, what brings you out so early today?" she asked him.

"Do you mind if we talk about the funeral arrangements we made together?" he replied.

"Any aspect in particular?" Denise teased.

"Well, yes," he continued. "What did they mean when they first asked you if the funeral had been paid for in advance?"

Denise smiled. "That's been bugging you ever since it was mentioned," she remarked, not quite sure where the conversation was heading. "Have you not heard of pre-payment plans?"

"Yes", he replied. "Peter used to tell me about them, but I am not sure whether he thought they were a good idea or not."

Denise's expression changed. "He had very strong feelings about it. In fact we both had."

"Do you mind telling me about them?" Bob was curious now, but he knew he was asking Denise to talk about something that was quite painful.

"I'll tell you how Peter felt about it and then you can make your own mind up," she answered.

To Shed A Light

"Peter worked for more than thirty years in the trade and during that time saw many changes take place in the industry, but the one change that he regretted more than anything else, was the introduction of pre-payment plans. If you were to talk to him about pre-arranging a funeral, that was different. He believed that was the best thing anyone could do, but the idea of paying for it in advance was repulsive to him."

"But surely that is a good thing too, easing the burden for the relatives who are left?" Bob interjected.

"In theory, yes, but not necessarily in practice," she continued. "Peter used to say that at one time, it was enough to do an excellent job of the highest standard in order to impress the client and thus ensure that your reputation was enhanced. The better the performance, the more satisfied people were, which in turn encouraged the staff to do an even better job. There was a difference between funeral directors in the area and good reasons why the customer would select one Company as opposed to another. Premises, vehicles, personalities, type of service, and style were all important features, and although all those differences still exist, and are still as important as ever, to some extent, pre-payment plans have taken away the customer's choice regarding the funeral director which means that these differences cannot be analysed."

"But surely you can still select the funeral director that you want?" asked Bob.

"Sometimes," Denise continued. "But if you have selected a pre-payment plan from a newspaper advertisement, you could be dealing direct with the plan provider, thus eliminating the need to contact or even select a funeral director. This will be done on your behalf, which is fine if you happen to choose the right plan, but if the funeral director you want operates a different type of pre-payment plan, he may not be allowed to accept your instructions for the funeral."

"So all you have to do is select the funeral director first, and then he will sell you his plan and he can also carry out the funeral when the time comes," said Bob enthusiastically.

"Absolutely right!" said Denise.

"So where's the problem?" asked Bob.

133

To Shed A Light

"The majority of funeral directors are not financial advisers and neither would they wish to be. Peter would not have been able to advise you whether one sort of pre-payment plan was more suited to your circumstances than another, so you may be selecting a funeral director but this way you are forced to have the only plan he is allowed to sell." Denise was almost on her soapbox now.

"So what was Peter's answer to all this? said Bob, now more confused than ever.

"All Peter wanted was to make sure that the customers had an opportunity to investigate the pre-payment plans that existed with a view to selecting the one that best suited their requirements, and then choose the funeral director that met the same criteria and then everyone would be happy. The family would be able to plan ahead for both the service they wanted and the best way of paying for it, based on their individual circumstances."

"So is that not possible? Asked Bob.

"Unfortunately not," said Denise. "Peter was annoyed that the Government had investigated the different types of pre-payment plan available, but then had stopped short of doing anything useful about them. Having spent a lot of time and money looking at the whole subject he thought they had wasted an opportunity. I suppose it would have been politically unpopular at the time. Either that, or they had failed to recognise the importance of customer choice in these different areas."

Bob almost said, "I only asked," realising by now that he had struck a nerve, but decided against it. Instead he went back to what Denise had said about pre-arrangements.

"So what is the difference between pre-payment and pre-planning, if Peter was happy about that aspect?"

"Peter was a great believer in arranging a funeral that satisfied the needs of the family at the time, but he also knew, and often said, that people were too upset once the death had occurred, to think clearly about what they wanted, so they invariably ended up arranging the type of funeral that most people have. If Peter had had his way, all funerals would be pre-arranged and the details recorded, possibly in a last will and testament and the arrangements would be planned before the client had a death in the family to worry about. All the options could be discussed, the premises and vehicles inspected and the funeral priced, but without the need for money to change hands. In this way, the funeral director could do what he is good at, and the client could approach someone more experienced in financial matters, for advice about how they should provide for such an event in the future. It may be an insurance policy, it may be a pre-payment plan, it may be stocks and shares, but equally, there are a lot of people about who cannot afford to contemplate the finances involved with arranging a funeral, and who may have to rely on financial help from the Government. They would still benefit from discussing their wishes in advance."

Bob felt that Denise was having a dig at him now, but she was not. It was only his guilt over the way in which my funeral had been arranged first time round. She could see he felt uncomfortable and guessed why, but chose not to put him out of his misery. After all, he had brought the subject up.

"Shall we change the subject?" said Bob, rather wisely in the circumstances.

"Good idea," she replied. "Do you have anything else in mind?"

"Well only just to say that I know you will be going to select a memorial for Peter's grave soon, and I just wondered if I could come with you, when you are ready," he asked.

"As long as you let me do the talking," she joked.

"I deserved that," he replied. "Are you ready for another coffee?" he said.

"Go on then," she laughed, "but then I am going to throw you out. I have a lot to do later."

Denise was left to reflect on the conversation she had just had with Bob, and realised how difficult it is to communicate some of those concerns to members of the public, especially when they are unaware of the difficulties that exist and whose only aim is to lighten the burden for those left behind. Had it not been for the fact that Bob had been there when the question was asked, he too would have been ignorant of these problems. Even now she was not convinced that the subject had been aired sufficiently and this was partly due to the fact

To Shed A Light

that he had caught her off-guard. Luke walked in just after Bob had left.

"What was that all about?" he asked.

"You know Bob," Denise answered. " He has been itching to ask me about pre-payment plans since we arranged the funeral and chose today to tackle the subject".

"I hope you put him right," he said.

"Well I thought I had until he had left and now I am not so sure."

"So what are you unhappy about then?" asked Luke.

"We did not talk about the difficulties that the funeral directors were likely to encounter in a few years time, as a result of pre-payment plans and there are a couple of major problem areas that, as far as I am concerned, Bob has not considered. Whether funeral directors are comfortable with the idea of pre-payment or not, the plans are probably here to stay and there will be a reduction in market share for those who have decided that the idea will not 'take off', or for those who simply hope that the problem will go away. The funerals will still happen, and will be dealt with by the funeral directors who at the time the plans were purchased, agreed to accept them. This will mean that the funeral director who is instructed by the plan provider to carry out the funeral, may not reside in the locality and the bereaved may have to travel further to make use of their chapel of rest and other facilities.

The funeral director will also receive a reduced amount for the funeral from the plan provider when the death occurs, because the price agreed at the time of taking out the plan will be a far cry from the amount required to provide the same standard and type of funeral by the time the service is required, always assuming of course, that the funeral director is still in existence. The people I know who have analysed the whole idea of pre-payment, have invariably ended up with more questions than answers but for those funeral directors who have lived without them for many years, only time will tell whether or not their fears are unfounded." Denise replied.

"I think it is a good thing Bob left when he did. You can put your soapbox away again. Besides, I don't suppose Bob is remotely interested in the welfare of the funeral directors or their market share for that matter. He is just concerned about the bereaved," said Luke.

"Stuff and nonsense!" Denise was getting angry. "A five minute chat about pre-payment plans doesn't give Bob Pritchett enough information to even begin to analyse the benefits for the bereaved. You know that Peter and I have lived with these wretched plans for the last decade and we have been torn about who really does benefit, ever since they were first muted. Had they been introduced purely to give peace of mind to the bereaved, we would have been the first to acknowledge it, but we have always seen it as pure commercialism, with profit for the plan providers, guaranteed funerals for those funeral directors belonging to the schemes and very little benefit for those who are really in need, and as for my soapbox, let us talk about something else and then I can put it away". They smiled at each other, realising that the day could have started off better than this.

"Bob has offered to accompany me to Henshaw's when I go to sort out the memorial," Denise said.

"What do you think. Is that what you really want?" Luke frowned.

"Well not really," Denise continued, "but I have already told him that he can come along on the understanding that he lets me do the talking."

"Do you know what you want?"

"Well, not exactly," replied Denise. "I am open to suggestions if you have any, although I have a fairly good idea."

"You sort it then," said Luke, "after all, it will be for you as well when the time comes." He smiled, not quite sure how Denise would react to that, but she saw the funny side of that too, and just grinned back.

It was in fact another two months before Denise finally decided to deal with the memorial, and only then because she was upset with the way the grave had looked on her last visit. Having had a while to get used to the idea of being without me by her side, selecting a memorial should be easier than the experience of making the funeral arrangements, especially as this has been her function at the office for a few years now. Dealing with the whole question of bereavement on a daily basis and organising all aspects of it for the benefit of the

To Shed A Light

bereaved, as stressful as that may be sometimes, is generally made easier by the fact that those involved do not know the family or the deceased. Talking about the text for the inscription on a memorial, for instance, is easy, until you are trying to apply those thoughts to someone you love, and the time that has elapsed between my funeral and this decision to sort the memorial out, will not have made the slightest difference. In this respect, Bob's input might be quite valuable and Denise had also realised this. In spite of her telling him that she would be doing all the talking, she had since decided to let him help her to select the stone, and with this in mind, telephoned Bob and asked him to call round to discuss how they should go about it. Bob, still smarting from the disastrous funeral arrangements he had made, was anxious not to make a fool of himself a second time, but also appreciated the fact that Denise was still prepared to have him tag along. By the time Bob arrived, Denise had formed a plan.

"What would you do if I was not here, in order to set about purchasing a memorial?" Denise asked.

"Probably write or telephone for some brochures," Bob replied.

"Well, in that case, I suggest that you do just that," she said.

"But surely you will want to use Henshaw's for the memorial, as you work there, and as you also sell memorials on a daily basis, is it not a bit unnecessary, going through the rigmarole of contacting others?"

"I doubt very much if we will be going elsewhere for the memorial," Denise continued, "but I would feel more comfortable about the whole thing if you too, were convinced that our final decision had been based on comprehensive, unbiased information."

"Surely the other memorial masons in the area will know you anyway," Bob suggested.

"Exactly," replied Denise, "which is where you come in, Bob."

"I got out of my depth last time," he said, worried about the direction in which they were moving. "I wouldn't want that to happen again."

"This time it will be different, Bob." she said enthusiastically. "This time, I will be one of the retailers that you will be contacting, and I will try to sell a memorial to you that you will be pleased with. The other memorial masons in the area will do the same exercise, and then at the end of the day, we can make a choice based on the options you have been given."

"I like that idea," Bob said. "Shall I write to them and ask for some brochures to start with?"

"Yes, do that, and then we will meet again to compare the brochures."

"I wonder what sort of help we will get from Barklett's, this time." Bob wondered out loud.

"None whatsoever!" was Denise's immediate reply. "Peter was always happy with funeral directors being involved with selling memorials, as long as they have a memorial side to the business where the memorial is actually produced. He would have kittens if he thought that I would have anything to do with them otherwise."

At this point Denise drifted off into her own thoughts, reflecting on the naivety of Bob's last statement. For many years, stonemasons have produced the memorial, having direct contact with the bereaved about this aspect, but in more recent years, for a variety of reasons, the sale of the memorial has become for some funeral directors, as important a part of his income, as the funeral itself. In some cases, this has led to a closer relationship between the two experts, the funeral director using all his sensitivity to talk to the bereaved about the memorial designs and the restrictions imposed by the various authorities, the costs incurred and all the other vital information which enables the customer to select the right memorial, and working with the memorial mason who in turn uses his expertise to convert those instructions into a memorial of lasting beauty. For others, the climate is not so rosy and there are funeral directors selling standard memorials direct from a catalogue, without the expert guidance or the skill of a memorial mason to produce the finished headstone. The memorial mason is naturally resentful of this approach, partly because of his lost income and partly because he knows that the bereaved are not getting

To Shed A Light

the best service available. There are still other funeral directors that have a memorial department, employing the skills from both trades to produce the finished memorial. Denise was just thinking that the two trades desperately needed each others support and co-operation in order to offer the bereaved a high standard of service, when Bob brought her down to earth again.

"I've got the message," said Bob. "I will only contact the stonemasons and the funeral directors who are also memorial masons or who have a proper masonry department."

It was about a fortnight later when Bob telephoned to say that he had received all the brochures he had asked for, and he was about to learn another lesson. He called round to share his thoughts with Denise.

"How did you get on?" Denise asked.

"Alright really," Bob replied. "There are so many to choose from and the prices vary enormously, which reminds me, I noticed you held your price list back, presumably until you have seen the others?"

"On the contrary, Bob, we have sent you what we send to everyone. A comprehensive brochure selection, a letter explaining why there is no price list included, and an invitation to contact us again if we can be of any help."

"Well all the other memorial masons have included theirs with the brochure." replied Bob.

"Then I think, as the next stage, you go through the brochures, without me being present, and choose something that you believe is appropriate for Peter's grave, and then we can have another chat," suggested Denise.

Two weeks elapsed, and still Denise had not heard another word from Bob, so she decided to telephone him to see how he was getting on. She established that he was close to a decision, having found it much harder than he thought, and they arranged to meet the following week. Denise suspected that this was likely to be a brief encounter, but she was not in a hurry for the memorial to be in place. She was comforted by the fact that they were dealing with it in their own way, and therefore felt relaxed.

"Have you decided then, Bob?" Denise asked.

To Shed A Light

"I have," he replied confidently. "Furthermore, I have chosen some suitable words for the inscription and I think you will approve."

"Show me the design first," Denise answered.

He showed her a photograph of an all polished black granite book from one of the brochures. He then produced a sheet of notepaper on which he had made copious notes about the durability of the stone, the size, the gilded letters and other factors that he felt Denise would be impressed with. Denise did not respond immediately, but then eventually said, "You had better read me the inscription."

He got as far as, "In ever loving memory of a dearly loved husband," and she stopped him.

"I am sorry, Bob, but we cannot have it." She felt sorry for him, but couldn't help but smile. "Has it taken you a long while to select that design?

"You know it has," he said, disgruntled, but not really surprised. "Look, before you dismiss it, let me explain why I chose this particular design." He continued before Denise could object." You know Peter was writing a book before he died, and whether or not it would ever have been good enough to publish, I thought that this would be appropriate. I also know that you read books 'like they are going out of fashion' and therefore thought it would be fitting for you too, which is also important."

"Bob, I did not say that I did not like it. In many ways it is appropriate, although it would not be my choice. I said that we cannot have it, therefore whether or not I like it, is irrelevant."

"What do you mean, we cannot have it?" said Bob.

"The churchyard regulations will not allow an all polished black granite memorial."

"I have seen one in the churchyard," retorted Bob.

"So have I, but that does not mean that it is allowed. At some point, probably during an interregnum that memorial was erected without permission and no-one has had the courage to tell the bereaved family to replace it with what was originally approved by the vicar. You are not the first person to feel cheated about that but only unpolished memorials are allowed. To add salt to your wounds, books are

141

To Shed A Light

not allowed either and just in case you're not smarting enough already, you need about three books to accommodate the inscription you have chosen." At this point, Denise burst out laughing, apologising as she did so. At first Bob was offended, but then he too smiled and as he listened to Denise, whose laugh is contagious, could not help but join in and before long they were both helpless without really knowing why they were laughing.

"There are lots of designs in the brochures that are not allowed in that case," said Bob after he had composed himself.

"The problem with all brochures, Bob, is that they can only give you a guide as to what is available. They are not really meant to do the job of selling the memorial and the advice you need in order to make a decision has to come from the experts, not from some glossy catalogue."

"Is that why you do not include a price list with your brochure?" Bob asked.

"One of the reasons, anyway. Give me all the brochures you have, and I'll go through them and cross off those which are not allowed, which will help you to think again," Denise said. "Avoid hearts, crosses, white marble and anything that exceeds the sizes I have written down here," she continued.

"That does not leave much," Bob argued.

"Do not feel disheartened about what seems to be a lack of choice. Think about what is allowed rather than what is forbidden and you will find that there is still a vast range to choose from. I am not over keen on the memorials that are not allowed anyway," she said.

Bob was realising already that there was more to selecting the memorial than he imagined and he had only considered the colour and shape so far. He knew that he was going to arrive at the stage where he would ask for Denise's help, but in the meantime, he was determined to get somewhere near a decision without assistance.

He took Denise's advice and looked more positively at the choice available. He also realised that there were other designs available, which were not depicted in the brochures. He also remembered the days when I used to speak to him about the memorials that are produced especially for the exhibitions. They too were not included in the literature. Bob decided to

To Shed A Light

use the pamphlets purely as a guide and started to visualise a memorial made up of several aspects of various designs. This would enable him to design his own memorial and was easily achieved. He was not sure what he wanted, but there were certain features he definitely did not want. Ignoring the material that the memorial was to be made of, dismissing all the shapes and carvings he disliked, he eventually came up with a couple of alternatives and decided that there was no need to make a final decision. Besides, ultimately, that was to be Denise's choice, not his, so he did not worry too much, realising that she probably had certain pre-determined ideas about the memorial. He smiled as he looked at his choices now, as they were so far adrift from his original thoughts. Having had to re-think because of what seemed to be restrictive regulations, had now given him an opportunity to find out what he really wanted without being too focused on any of the standard brochure designs. He was surprised that his designs were not more elaborate than they were. He looked again at the sketches he had made and still confirmed in his own mind that simplicity in style did not detract from the elegance of the memorial. He knew now, but probably would not say, why Denise was so unhappy with his initial choice of a book, and also realised that pointed in a different direction, he too had changed his mind completely. He was also satisfied that his lengthy epitaph would now fit on the new design, there being much more space to accommodate it. He was only really unsure now about which side to have the flower container so decided to air Denise's views on this aspect, before presenting his final designs for her approval. He telephoned her, and arranged to meet her for coffee to discuss his thoughts so far. The next morning, they were sitting in a café, watching the rain beating against the window as they discussed Bob's thoughts. He decided not to mention the progress he had made, but just to ask for her ideas about the flower container. As Bob had made no decision about this aspect, it was easier for Denise to discuss it.

"Would it make your task easier or more difficult if I tell you that I would prefer not to have a container at all?" Denise said.

To Shed A Light

"It would make it easier, because my only thoughts to date have been on where it should be within the design, not whether or not we needed one at all. At the end of the day, though, I would prefer to think that the design I have chosen would be able to accommodate all your requirements." Bob said.

"The next time you go to a cemetery, have a look at the number of memorials that have empty flower containers sitting in their holders or are missing altogether. Then ask yourself, as I have so often in the past, whether or not that has any bearing on the way in which the relatives of the deceased feel about the person who has been buried. It may give an indication about how frequently the grave is visited, but I feel that the sight of an empty vase is far worse than a memorial without the provision in the first place." Denise said, her eyes full of sadness as she spoke. "It will not stop me putting flowers on Peter's grave, or visiting as often as I want, but if there is no vase there, no-one will be surprised to find that there are no flowers either, and I cannot bear the thought of plastic flowers."

Bob was surprised, but also quite pleased. It had not occurred to him to question the need for a vase at all. He had almost finished his coffee, and felt that he had sufficient information to enable him to complete the design and was talking in those terms when Denise interrupted.

"I realise from the way you are talking that we are near to choosing the memorial that we want, but there is one other consideration before you present your final drawing for approval." Denise said with that look in her eye that worried Bob. He wondered what bombshell she was about to drop.

"What is that?" he asked.

"If there is to be no container for flowers, there will be no need for a base for the headpiece to fix to, which means that the headstone could be fixed straight into the ground, eliminating the need for any of the more modern ground anchors to secure the memorial," Denise replied.

"Most of the memorials I have looked at have a matching base of some description, even if they do not have a hole to accommodate the flower container. Isn't it going to look odd without one?" Bob replied. Denise, suspecting that she may have touched a nerve, smiled reassuringly at Bob.

"Forget what most people do," Denise continued. "The majority of people do not even get to discuss the fixing of the memorial, but with health and safety considerations it is more important now than it has ever been. Anyway, if you have a look in a traditional churchyard, you will see many memorials that have been fixed in this more traditional manner, and most of them will be really old and still firmly in the ground. Compare these with some of the more modern memorials that have been fixed with bases and concrete plinths and you will see what I mean." Bob was not too disappointed, because as he thought about the implications of what Denise was saying, he also realised that it would make very little difference to his design. In fact, the simplicity of the design would probably be enhanced with this method of fixing, he was just frustrated that he knew so little about the subject and seemed to need guidance at every step. He could not believe how complicated it was to organise and yet so satisfying in another. The more he thought about what he was doing, the more thrilled he became at the prospect of doing this last thing for me, and he knew how important it was. The fact that Denise had trusted him so far made him wary of the outcome. He thought that at any moment she would dismiss all his efforts and say, "This is what we are going to have!" But she did not.

Bob had been in contact with the other stonemasons at various stages who had confirmed much of what Denise had said, but they had only answered his questions and had not really given him the guidance he sought. The method of fixing the memorial had not been broached by anyone else at this stage. When Bob had returned to his drawing board to complete the design, he found it easier than he thought. He merely rubbed out the bases, added the height to the headstone, for this is all it was now, and his efforts were finished. He carefully typed the inscription in the space on his drawing and waited for the opportunity to present it to Denise. His opportunity came the next day, when Denise, also anxious to see what he had done, invited him round to talk it through with her.

To Shed A Light

It was taller than she had thought it would be, and wider too, but it was not unlike the design that she had in mind herself. It had a round top and chamfered front edges and no other carvings. Denise was pleased. She wondered whether she had unwittingly steered him in this direction, so near to her own thoughts was the design now, compared with the original 'book' memorial, but decided that Bob had perhaps considered all the alternatives and had hopefully taken on board some of her wishes too. In fact, for once, Bob had not tried to impose his own ideas, but had listened to Denise, remembered some of the conversations that we had had in the past, and put it all together to arrive at the final result. There remained just two aspects to conclude. One was the wording for the inscription and the second, equally as important, was the material that the memorial should be made of. The first was easier than Bob thought, but again, he was surprised.

"Why do we have a stunningly simple design for the headstone, and then cram it with words that are so artificial and not written in the language that we used every day?" asked Denise.

"What particular aspect are you referring to? Bob asked.

"In ever loving memory of a dearly loved husband," she said.

"Well he was!" Bob replied.

"That is not in question," Denise continued. "We need to consider the reason for erecting the memorial in the first place. Peter and I had similar views about this so I am fairly comfortable about it. We are erecting the memorial because it enables us to mark the grave and we would not be doing so unless we loved him, so there is no real need to put 'In loving memory of' as the first line. Those who knew him are aware of his attributes, and his failings for that matter, and those who never knew him, will not be remotely interested in what we say on the stone. There is not enough room to say all the things I would love to say, and that is why I think that just his name, followed by the year he was born and the year he died, will suffice. That will provoke all the memories in those who visit his grave." She had nearly finished, but she wanted to say one more thing to Bob before he had his two pennyworth.

To Shed A Light

"The fewer the words, the larger they can be, and this will mean that the letters can be carved more deeply, and will therefore last longer, and will also be seen clearly from a greater distance. This simple inscription will enhance the memorial and will also surprise a lot of people. There will also be plenty of room for a similarly appropriate second inscription when it is my turn."

Now it was Bob's turn to be pleased. He was delighted that she was happy with his design and the inscription, having thought about it, will do justice to the memorial. He had often thought how unnecessarily flowery some of the inscriptions seemed to be, but he never thought of simplifying it. This feeling that it is necessary to conform to what is usually done, is a terrific barrier to overcome.

"So what about the stone itself?" enquired Bob.

"You know we cannot have white marble or highly polished granite," Denise replied. "What we need to do next is the same exercise that you did with the design. Forget what is not allowed, and concentrate your efforts on the types of stone that are acceptable. Think about what we are trying to achieve and ensure that it is still going to be there in many years to come." Denise was trying to motivate Bob again.

"Perhaps I should get some samples of the material for comparison," Bob suggested.

"You could do," said Denise. "But do not forget that this will only show you what the memorial will look like when it is new. I would have a look in the local churchyards and see how some of the memorials have survived over the years, if I were you," Denise replied.

"I will do that and then ask you to identify the type of stone that seems to last the longest without deteriorating," said Bob.

"Remember that all stone weathers, which is slightly different to deteriorating, Bob. Make sure that you are happy with the changes that will inevitably occur and then you will not be disappointed with the changes over the years." Denise replied.

When Bob left Denise this time, it was with a good heart for he felt that he had accomplished a great deal. Selecting the material was all that was left to do, and then the memorial

To Shed A Light

could be ordered, so he was feeling pretty smug. It was several days before Bob finally got back to Denise and he had a couple of alternatives in mind. It is true to say that Denise at this stage had already decided on the material, so when one of Bob's suggestions turned out to be black Slate, she felt quite relieved. It was an easy matter to convince Bob that this would be the ideal material for the memorial and this was easily followed with a decision to have the letters hand-cut and left untouched. Having gone so far, Denise helped Bob out with the fine-tuning of the order. The style of letter, the insurance for the memorial and the initial preparation of the grave were all agreed and the order placed. Bob on this occasion had done well, but he breathed a sigh of relief as he went to sleep that night. He had no idea he could feel so excited about something that was so upsetting, and yet he was looking forward now to seeing the memorial in place. Never again will he see a memorial on a grave without acknowledging the heartache that was probably experienced in the purchasing of it.

It was four months later when the memorial was in place and the grave planted. Bob's first visit to the grave after this was a shock. Having looked forward so much to seeing his efforts achieve fruition, he had not considered the impact of seeing the words in place on the memorial and the effect they would have on him. He was delighted with the stone, but devastated by the memories it evoked, so how, he wondered, would Denise cope with this experience? With mixed feelings was the answer. She went alone at first and then took Luke and Jane along for her second visit. She was not really sure whether she had asked them along for her sake or theirs and they had similar misgivings, but they supported each other nevertheless and felt able after that to go independently of each other, should they feel the need to visit the grave again. This was just another hurdle, another experience which had been overcome, but it did not make subsequent visits any easier to bear.

What more can they do, but to carry on with their lives, thinking of me occasionally, wrestling with their torment at other times, and sometimes enjoying a well deserved peace of mind?

Bob had learned more about bereavement and its affect upon those who are left, in the period since my death, than he could possibly have imagined, but he still had a few thoughts and some nagging doubts.

Chapter Eleven

In spite of Denise's willingness to overlook the problems that Bob had experienced with the arrangements for my funeral initially, Bob still felt uneasy, and to some extent, annoyed that it could have happened. With hindsight, he knew that he should have gone to Henshaw's in the first place, but at the time he was too upset and not really thinking as clearly as he would normally. Given that he had chosen the wrong establishment, he also realised that he had paid little attention to the complexity of what he was undertaking and also realised, that in selecting Barklett's as the funeral director he had given no advance thought whatsoever to the type of service he would receive or the facilities that were available. Conscious now that this is probably true of most people when they arrange a funeral, he decided to find out, without involving Denise, what he could have done to avoid this awkward situation. He knew already the difference between Barklett's and Henshaw's, but decided in his own mind that they must have been influenced to some extent by the fact that I had worked there for so long, and therefore decided that the service they received from Henshaw's was better than it would have been otherwise. He had no way of knowing that, but what he could do, was to set about planning the details of his own funeral in order that his family would be spared the same anxieties. This would also enable him to compare the services available in his area, but he needed to know what to look for. Until now, it had never occurred to him that there was any difference between one funeral director and another. He had also determined not to compare the costs at an early stage, for he thought it best to establish his requirements first, compare the means of providing the service he wanted and then he could more easily analyse the price and the various means available to pay for it. He would also consider the idea of pre-payment.

He made a list of all the factors that were important to him, based on his recent experience, and listing them in order of priority, was surprised to find himself putting 'care' at the top of his list. He was not only referring to the care for the family and the person who has died, but realised that he wanted to be looked after too, especially when it came to guidance and advice over his perceived requirements. At this stage, he realised that he would also need some idea of what he wanted in the way of funeral arrangements and that he would have to record those instructions somewhere if he expected his family to adhere to these wishes. Making his last will and testament was something that Bob had put off for years, and yet now he felt that it was the right approach. As he realised that these instructions should include the funeral arrangements, he decided to wait until after he had finished his analysis of funeral directors. He remembered also, that I had made my wishes known in my will, and this was not referred to immediately. He wondered how many people should be made aware of his instructions in order to be certain that they would be honoured when the time comes.

When Bob was working at the bank, he and I had been on a general management course, part of which had included 'mind-mapping' as a means of analysing a problem. At the time, Bob did not appear to be very enthusiastic about the technique, partly because he was due for his early retirement and was therefore reluctant to learn new skills, and partly because he was not the type to get excited about new ideas. Nevertheless, he decided to convert his thoughts now into a mind-map, before going any further. This was the first time he had used the idea since the course and he was sceptical about the results, even though he could see the logic to this approach. First he concentrated on the map itself and then added the text to the branches, detailing all his requirements as he thought more about them.

He did not try to do it all in one session, for the beauty of the mind map was the fact that he could return to it at any time and add the different items as they occurred to him. When he had achieved what he thought was sufficient to enable him to visit the funeral directors in his locality, he printed out the text of his map:-

Selecting A Funeral Director

1. Care
Doing exactly what is required to enable the funeral to take place is not enough. From the lessons learned from Peter's funeral, it is obvious that funeral directors are dealing with people who are not only vulnerable, but who are also absolutely helpless and unfamiliar with all that needs to be achieved in a relatively short period. They are also trying to arrange a funeral that will satisfy the needs of those who are not able to organise the details, but who will be seeking comfort from the funeral itself. Ordering the right number of vehicles and choosing the coffin is relatively straight-forward, but the advice given to help me arrive at the right decision in my particular circumstances, is more important than anything else. Guidance over the options available and being nurtured along gently, in an unhurried manner, will impress me more than the routinely efficient service that only deals with the essentials and in a completely business-like manner. Certainly I want the administration to be dealt with efficiently and with precision, but not while I am there to witness the obvious need for organisation. I want everyone I come into contact with, no matter what their role, to be nice to me every step of the way because that will ease my burden more than anything else. It would certainly be an improvement on my last experience. The care for everyone involved, should also be reflected in the quality of service generally, for the peripheral services which may be available for my convenience will only be of value, if they are geared to provide the best that is available in that field. I am happy to organise everything under one roof, but I hate the 'supermarket' approach, so I will look for quality of service in each of the areas, dealing with outside sources for anything which is not up to scratch.

2. Vehicles
The funeral director I select must have a fleet of matching vehicles, whether or not they have a policy of hiring additional vehicles from other sources at busy times, because this will indicate the standard of service they wish to portray. I will also insist on their own vehicles being used, wherever possible,

To Shed A Light

for my funeral. There seems little point in selecting a funeral director because his vehicles are impressive, if he then has to hire inferior vehicles from elsewhere in order to carry out my funeral.

2.1 Cleanliness
To a certain extent, I do not mind what type of vehicles they run, as long as they match, are in a good state of repair and spotlessly clean inside and out, and I shall want to inspect the vehicles before placing an order with anyone. The driver's cab will certainly tell me how things really are in the cleanliness department.

2.2 Make and model
I have an open mind about the make and model of vehicles used, but they must not be older than eight years and must be practical in terms of getting in and out.

3. Staff

3.1 Telephone manner
There is nothing worse than having a telephone conversation with someone who obviously wants to be doing something different. This is true in all walks of life, but I do not think I could tolerate an unsympathetic voice at this time, so I shall monitor their initial approach carefully to see how I am handled, especially when they realise that there is a possibility that I may go elsewhere. My routine enquiry will no doubt be unwelcome if they are particularly busy at the time, but perhaps that is just my cynicism. I remember receiving a booklet from the Registrar's office, explaining what to do when someone dies, but it was too detailed to analyse at the time. I really wanted someone to take charge of me, and tell me exactly what to do in order to arrange the funeral. This time it will be different.

3.2 Dress
I am a traditionalist, so I shall expect to see the office staff wearing a respectable uniform, and the funeral staff wearing pinstripe trousers, black jackets and waistcoats. I was

impressed with Henshaw's turnout and especially the tailed coat worn by the person in charge on the day so I shall consider that to be the standard to set.

3.3 Number qualified
I had also noticed in Henshaw's, the certificates on the wall relating to the staff qualifications. Some were for embalming, some had their diploma in funeral directing, some were certificates of advanced driving and there may have been others I had not noticed. I am not sure which gave me more comfort, the certificates on the wall in the offices or the paintings in the waiting room. To some extent, the array of certificates gave me a feeling of security but I remember feeling at one stage that they were "blowing their own trumpet" a little. Why not, if they are good at what they do? In contrast, the paintings made me feel more relaxed, so I suppose a balance between the two is ideal. However, whether or not the certificates are on view, it is important to me that people become qualified and the advanced driving qualification impressed me because I had not come across it before.

3.4 Part-time
I am now beginning to realise that all funeral directors employ part-time staff at some time or other, and I do not have a problem with that, but there is one proviso. They must wear the same uniform and operate the same quality of service. That might be a tall order! Staff employed on a part-time basis can be trained to the same standard as full-time employees, whereas those hired from other funeral establishments will be trained in a different way, to reflect a different approach. Their uniforms too, may be different.

3.5 Drivers
The only significant item to note here is that the drivers, who should all be dressed the same, must be of similar height because there is nothing worse than watching a coffin being carried awkwardly at a funeral. I remember Peter telling me about a trip he made to France once where he visited another funeral director. They had a rack of brand new clothing in

readiness for new members of staff. He asked them how they could know with certainty in advance, that the suits would fit new applicants, as they were all the same size. The response was simple. "If the clothes do not fit, they do not get the job!" I have always remembered this and shall now use this measure for my analysis.

3.6 Funeral Directors
I would like to think that the person who arranges the funeral would also be responsible for officiating on the day. I know that this does not always happen and in times of sickness it is wise to have another funeral director who is familiar with the arrangements, but I shall certainly ask the question.

3.7 Training
I have seen funerals taking place at the crematorium, and it is fairly obvious who has been trained and who has not. I realise in spite of the copious notes I am making about my requirements, that I am going to be hard pressed to find a way, let alone the time, to do a sufficiently detailed analysis of every funeral director in the area. I am also aware that I am probably being over-optimistic if I expect to find perfection at any of the establishments in the locality, but at least I can get a feel about the style and standard of service available, which would be an improvement on my last performance.

4. Premises

4.1 Embalming facilities
I realise that saying "goodbye" to Peter was an extremely important occasion as far as Denise was concerned and because of the delay between the time of death and the funeral, and the fact that Denise wanted him at home, it was only possible because he had been embalmed. Prior to this, I had been unaware of the advantages of embalming, if indeed I ever even considered it. I am now convinced that it is worthwhile, and will need no persuading by the funeral director concerned. This means that it is up to me to establish that they have embalming facilities and qualified staff available, and that they are as enthusiastic about it as I am

now. Prior to Peter's death I would have squirmed at the thought of it and I am surprised that something which I found so repulsive only a short time ago, has now become an important consideration.

4.2 Decor
At one time, I would scarcely have noticed the decoration in an office and I doubt if it would have influenced my decision about dealing with the company, but the environment was more important when it came to arranging the funeral and is an aspect that I had not considered. Initially, because I was asked to wait longer at Barklett's than I wanted to, I was looking at the decor and analysing it to a far greater extent than I would have done, had I been dealt with immediately. Now, with hindsight, I feel that the style of furniture and general decor was as shabby as the overall care I received. It occurs to me that unless the funeral directors I approach are amenable, they may deny me the opportunity to view the premises.

4.3 Waiting room
It was not just the decoration that offended me at Barklett's, because at the time I was oblivious to it, but the tacky outdated magazines were well thumbed and not really appropriate in view of the way I was feeling at the time. I found it difficult to concentrate on reading them when I was so nervous at the prospect of arranging a funeral for the first time. I do not know what to look for in this respect, so it would probably be better to make an appointment to see someone, thus eliminating the need to wait or to read any magazines. Sitting in the same room as others who were also upset, came as a shock and I felt uncomfortable. They probably felt the same, but if we had both been made aware in advance, it may have been better. I was never much good in that situation!

4.4 Toilet facilities
Have you ever noticed the lack of toilet facilities in a place where you are already nervous before you arrive? The degree of cleanliness in this department is also a good guide as to the standards elsewhere.

5. Services

The quality of service is more important than the number of options available, but my analysis of these additional services is intended to determine the funeral director's expertise in these areas rather than just list the fact that they are available. To some extent, they are secondary to the exercise because if I find a funeral director that outshines all others as far as quality of funeral service is concerned, but who has no additional services to offer, I shall go elsewhere for those peripheral services. At the end of the day, however, in order to make things as easy as possible for my relatives when the time comes, I would prefer to achieve as much as possible from one funeral establishment.

5.1 Information

I know that all funeral directors will give me sufficient information to enable me to arrange a funeral, but I want much more than that. This is probably the most important area because I feel that I was badly let down before. There was an assumption that I knew what I wanted and knew the right questions to ask, but I didn't. I wanted to be guided through every aspect with information that if anything, was superfluous to my requirements, rather than given the bare minimum. It is true to say that I may not have helped my own cause one iota, but I was too upset at the time to be good at what I was doing and this is what I regret most. At Barklett's, no-one seemed to acknowledge the difficulty I was in and had assumed that because I was not related to Peter, that I was also not as upset as I would otherwise have been. When I look at the different services available, therefore, I shall want to receive not just the information about the option itself, but also the reasons why the funeral itself would be enhanced if I were to take advantage of that particular service.

5.2 Range

To some extent, the range of services available will depend on the premises and the location, but it will also depend on the enthusiasm of the management and the ability of the staff to provide them. For instance, I do not know whether or not having the deceased at home prior to the funeral is an option that is available at Barklett's because it was never mentioned when I arranged Peter's funeral. It may well have been achieved had I asked for it, but it was something which would never have occurred to me. I wonder now what other services are available which I knew nothing about. At first, I was annoyed about it, but then I realised that all funeral directors are different and some will offer a wide range of additional services whereas others will only offer the basic requirements for a funeral, and it is this that will help me to decide who will satisfy my wishes best.

5.3 Flowers

Henshaw's were able to supply the flowers, and we were happy to use their service because they have their own florist. The quality of the tributes was superb, but if they had not been of the highest standard, I would have preferred to buy them elsewhere. Peter had a problem with funeral directors who recommended a particular florist to customers because it invariably reflected on the funeral director if anything went wrong and the florist, who produced the wonderful tribute, rarely received the credit. As far as my own funeral arrangements are concerned, I am not altogether bothered about the flowers, and I shall probably suggest donations to a charity rather than floral tributes, or at least give the mourners a choice. Nevertheless, I shall be interested to see how many funeral directors also sell and produce their own floral tributes in my area, and how the standard compares with the other florists in the town.

5.4 Memorials

Six months ago I knew absolutely nothing about memorials, and whilst the professional would still think that to be the case, I do believe that I have learned quite a lot recently. In one sense, the funeral director who has nothing to do with the sale of memorials has little incentive to broach the subject when making the arrangements for the funeral, and yet the place where the burial takes place, be it of the deceased where a normal burial is concerned, or cremated remains, will invariably dictate the style of memorial that will be allowed. In this respect, the funeral director can influence what sort

To Shed A Light

of memorial will be purchased, without even discussing the subject. His advice and information at an early stage are therefore vital if the relatives of the deceased are going to be happy with their choice of memorial. It will not be necessary for the funeral director to be conversant with all the memorials that are available, but it is essential that he understands the different types allowed in one section of a cemetery compared with another, when the decision is made about the burial. The memorial mason, whose sole aim in life is to sell the client the best memorial possible within the financial constraints of his client, can only do so, if the family have been correctly advised in the first place by the funeral director. When I arranged the memorial for Peter's grave, I did not understand this. I am not sure with hindsight whether the decision for his burial would have been any different, no matter how expert the funeral director was about memorials, for Peter had purchased his burial plot in advance of his funeral, but for me, it would be different. I have no pre-determined wishes and I welcome the advice that will enable me to decide on a burial or cremation and the other factors that stem from that decision. Whilst still easily influenced in this direction, I am leaning towards the idea of a traditional burial, and I would have been surprised if twelve months ago, someone were to suggest this as a possibility. I have been so fascinated by the different types of stone available and the wealth of designs to choose from, that the whole subject took on a different meaning for me. I welcomed the opportunity to do something positive at a time when in many other respects I felt so helpless. I had the advantage again, that Denise had a vested interest in the influence she had on my choice of memorial for Peter, but nevertheless, she was good at what she did and explained far more to me about the purchasing of a memorial than I thought possible and it was not just the production of the memorial that became important, but all the factors involved with the planning of it. Whilst I realise that this expertise can be learned by a funeral director, the control of the final production is also important to me, so the person who sells me the memorial, will also have to produce it.

5.4.1 Own workshop?

I was fascinated by Henshaw's memorial workshop, because it allowed input from the client in the final design and production. I remember while they were cutting the letters on Peter's memorial there was another customer on the premises, busily photographing the various stages of the production of his baby's memorial and I was impressed with the patience afforded to him during this time. He was delighted that he had been allowed to witness the work being carried out and in turn, the carver knew that his client would be satisfied with the result because of the ongoing consultation with him.

5.5 Catering

The last thing I would want to do is to organise the catering after the funeral. Unlike Peter, I do believe it is important to have folk back after the funeral for refreshments before they return home, and whilst neighbours often help in these circumstances, I cannot think of anyone who might volunteer. If the funeral director can organise this on my behalf, therefore, and as long as my family do not lose control of what will happen, I would be pleased to let them organise this, either at my own home or on their own premises.

5.5.1 On their own premises?

If a room has been set aside at the funeral directors for catering after the funeral, or even to provide a meeting place for mourners before the funeral commences, it must be large enough, furnished in a homely manner, and far enough away from the activities of the other funerals that are taking place, in order to avoid the noisy environment often experienced when relatives and friends meet for the first time in decades. The funeral director's premises will govern whether or not this is a good idea, so I shall reserve judgement for now.

5.6 Printing

I do not know who was responsible for the printing of the hymn sheets for Peter's funeral, or even if they were arranged direct with the printer, but a good deal of thought had gone into the production of them. I shall investigate this and

To Shed A Light

determine whether or not this should be left with the funeral director, the minister or my relatives to organise.

6. Location

Accessibility is extremely important for a funeral director's premises. When someone is upset, the last thing they want to do, is to drive round an unfamiliar town looking for the right place, but more importantly, it must be in a position which is conducive to the peaceful atmosphere which is expected. The site must also be large enough to accommodate all that is required for the services that are being offered, and preferably not trading alongside another business that would detract from the serenity of the funeral home.

6.1 Parking

Parking easily is important and having sufficient space to accommodate all the visitors at one time, especially when the assembly point is the funeral director's premises, can enhance the image no end.

7. Pre-payment plans available

If I intend to pay in advance for the funeral, and I am at the moment unsure about whether that is necessary or not, I will need to ask what plans are available at the funeral directors I visit. However, I need to be certain that the plan I select is the best of all pre-payment plans available and the only way I can determine this, is to do a separate analysis of pre-payment generally. I have already decided that my choice of funeral director will be more important than my choice of plan so if the funeral director I choose cannot provide the pre-payment plan I think best suits my requirements, I shall not pay for the funeral in advance. I am determined not to select a plan first and then find that I am pointed in the direction of a funeral director that cannot provide the standard of service I want.

8. Peripheral services advice

Denise was lucky enough to be aware of the help available for the bereaved after the funeral was over, but Cruse, S.A.N.D.S; Compassionate Friends and other similar organisations meant nothing to me. I had never heard of anyone using their services and was sceptical about the perceived benefits. Only with hindsight and seeing Denise in a state of bewilderment for what seemed to be an eternity, do I now realise the value of the work they do. It was never mentioned to Denise by anyone, and I can only assume that this was because she was chairman of the local branch of Cruse and therefore did not need the advice, but I wondered where the information came from for those who like me, knew absolutely nothing about it. Perhaps this is the role of the church? Perhaps the funeral director will advise me, although I cannot help thinking that I am expecting far too much. After all, at this point, all I want to do is to give instructions for my own funeral and it will be my relatives who will require this additional information, rather than me.

9. Reputation

Although I have lived in the area for many years, I had never needed the services of a funeral director until Peter died and therefore I was unaware of the differences between one funeral director and another. It is true to say, with hindsight, and from speaking to others since, that Henshaw's have a good reputation for a high standard of care and service but I spoke to no-one prior to his funeral about the funeral directors in the area. Once I have done my analysis and arranged my funeral details with whoever seems to be the best suited to my requirements, there is really no way of passing any useful information on to those who are also in need of a funeral director. Neither will anyone think to ask my opinion, for few will know what I have done. The analysis I am about to do is achievable because I am not emotionally involved, having no funeral to organise, in reality, at this time. If I was thinking about purchasing a car, I would happily visit many showrooms to determine who was going to offer the best service and aftercare at a price that was acceptable before making my decision. The car would be the same as long as my requirements did not alter but the company could make me feel a whole lot better if they did a better job than their competitors down the road. I would also be more inclined to talk about their help and efficiency, given the opportunity.

To Shed A Light

We do not normally do this exercise when arranging a funeral, neither do we talk comfortably about death and yet all funeral directors are different, possibly offering a similar service with similar results, but never identical.

10. Independent?

There has been a lot of discussion in recent years about the differences between the small independent or family businesses and the larger conglomerates, but my analysis will only address the service available at the different funeral homes, whether or not that service is delivered by the owner of the business or a branch manager, and the costs involved. If the company can meet all the criteria, I shall not worry about whose name is above the door, for I have no loyalty to any, although I must concede to a slight bias towards Henshaw's because of the service they performed for Peter's funeral. It only occurs to me now, that the only detail I was not involved with, was the pricing of the funeral, which quite rightly, was a matter between Denise and Adam.

Bob was now conscious of the fact that he could not just walk into someone's funeral establishment and act like the proverbial factory inspector. Certainly he needed to see the premises and he wanted to talk to the staff, but it was not his intention to catch them off-guard. He hoped that they would always be ready to receive visitors, but he remembered his banking days where he had received advance warning of an impending visit from the management team and he knew how that experience had affected him and the rest of the team. He suddenly had another thought. He would not be able to see the chapel of rest, without special arrangements being made for him to do so, because the relatives of anyone lying in there would not take kindly to some stranger appearing, just to have a look at the décor and style of the room. He would have to use a more professional approach and one which he hoped would enable the funeral directors to prepare for his visit with a view to impressing him with the service they offer. After all, that is all he is trying to achieve. So he wrote to the five establishments in the area, outlining his wishes and explaining that he wanted to arrange the details of his own funeral in

To Shed A Light

advance, but not necessarily paying for it. He smiled to himself as he realised that the written response he was to receive from each would go some way towards helping him to analyse the type of establishment it is. He could certainly see from the letter heading whether or not he was dealing with a family business, for the advertisements he had seen in the local newspaper gave no hint whatsoever. It was to be several days before he received the first response and by the end of the following week he had received a reply from all but one. The only funeral director who did not respond at all, was Barklett's, and Bob, although a little disappointed, realised that they would recognise his name and address from organising my funeral details and felt that in the circumstances, they probably preferred not to get involved. This left him with Henshaw's, Robert Laing & Sons, Dewbury and Fische Ltd. and Donald Harte & Sons. All were within an eight-mile radius of each other and were similar in size. No-one seemed unwilling to receive him or show him round but the letter he received from Henshaw's was different and more personal. In Adam's letter to him, he had acknowledged his recent bereavement and had indicated that it would be nice to see him again. Bob was surprised and pleased that he had written the letter himself, and felt less awkward about contacting him again. He still had, quite understandably, mixed feelings about the way he thought that he would be treated, but realised now that this was not going to be a problem. It had taken all of Bob's courage to include Henshaw's on his mailing list, but it was only his own guilt and that had now subsided.

Bob was amazed at the difference between the four funeral directors but was pleased at the end of his visits that he felt comfortable with all of them. Although incredibly helpful, Mr. Jacobs at Robert Laing & Sons was not as well qualified as the others and whilst his premises were adequate they lacked the finesse of the other three. In every other respect he was satisfied. Donald Harte saw Bob personally, which immediately gave them an edge, but the chapels were dowdy and old fashioned and had a fusty smell about them. The vehicles were clean and smart but that was more than could be said for the staff, who seemed to care little about their own appearance and were obviously not motivated by the need to welcome a visitor. The only two "in the running" therefore, were Henshaw's and Dewbury and Fische Ltd. In spite of Bob's bias, he had a lot of time for the welcome at Dewbury and Fische and learned a lot more there than he had at the other two. The premises were clean and tidy and not prepared just for his benefit. They obviously set a high standard and the staff help to maintain it. The vehicles were similar to Henshaw's and Bob was able to establish that they hire vehicles from each other where necessary. The chapel of rest was traditional in style, although Bob had not been too keen on the stained glass windows. The information given was comprehensive and it was difficult to differentiate between the two funeral directors in terms of expertise, care and facilities, although the embalming room at Dewbury and Fische Ltd. was extremely small and not used as often as it might be. They employed a 'trade embalmer' as opposed to having their own but they could easily have accommodated my wishes in this respect. Back at home, Bob was busy analysing the results of his visits, and was quite pleased that it had not been as difficult to achieve as he had originally envisaged. What impressed him most, however, was the additional information that had been volunteered by all of them, when not under pressure from a client to arrange a funeral quickly. Without exception, they were all happy to talk about a wide range of topics, some of which were helpful to Bob as far as his own requirements were concerned, whilst others were just for general interest. At one point, during a chat with Adam at Henshaw's, Bob was almost ready to donate his body for medical research, with the prospect of a free funeral, but due to the fact that they only seemed to accept perfect specimens, those who had not been autopsied or had not died from Cancer, changed his mind.

I was listening to Frank at Dewbury & Fische Ltd. explaining to Bob about repatriation for those who have died abroad, and I was able to relate to the experience that Denise and I had several years ago, when we went to Hungary by road.........

It was a perfectly normal Wednesday morning, with very little excitement in our lives and nothing spoiling at the weekend either and I was just a telephone call away from a

To Shed A Light

tragedy that was to change all that. It was about two years after my Romanian trip and the route through Hungary was still fresh in my mind. A lady who was desperate for help was making the telephone call from Hungary. Two of her relatives had been killed in an accident and she had neither the money nor the expertise to transport them back to this country and to their home town. Their insurance did not cover repatriation and they were at a loss to know what to do. In order to keep the expenses down, I had to achieve the repatriation without paying a fortune in overtime and overnight expenses for what was to be a four-day round trip. Denise, caught off-guard when I telephoned her and asked her to accompany me to Hungary, hastily made arrangements for her parents to look after Luke and Jane, and we set off in a hearse the next day, to collect the two accident victims. We took two zinc-lined coffins with us to save the expense of purchasing them in Hungary, although this was frowned upon by the funeral directors there. I had remembered the hospitality that was shown to us when we were accommodated by Rotarians in Scharding on the way back from Romania and decided that it would be nice to show Denise where we had stayed. We drove on with this in mind, but when we arrived at Scharding on what was a scorching hot day in August, there was a street party in progress. A hearse was not the most welcome sight, and we were ushered out of the town as quickly but as nicely as possible, by a local priest, whose English was as non-existent as my Austrian, but we got the message. We eventually found accommodation at a wonderful guest house in a nearby village, and hoped that we could hide the hearse to avoid being moved on again. The journey was long and hard and very tiring and the language barrier in Hungary did not help, but eventually, with a little help from the relatives in Hungary who could speak the language, we achieved our goal and returned to England.

Bob had been fascinated when he listened to Frank detailing the Consular requirements of different countries and although he was not remotely interested from a personal point of view, also realised that people can die anywhere, and it was nice to know that he could put the arrangements in the hands of those who could cope in any of these circumstances. Both Frank and Adam in their own different ways, chatted about all aspects of funeral arranging, and really only for Bob's benefit, went into far greater detail than they would have done normally.

My own tragic death has highlighted for Bob the fact that death is not something that always happens as a result of a long illness but listening to Adam describing some of the tragedies that he has dealt with over the years, he realises that my own death, as tragic as it was, has not been as traumatic as some of the deaths by suicide and murder that have also been a part of the lives of both these men in their occupations.

Throughout my career as a funeral director, I can honestly say that cases of suicide have been the most difficult in terms of stirring my own emotions, for I have always believed that help should be available for everyone in this day and age and listening to Adam describing to Bob what was for me the most heart rending experience of my career, even now in my coccooned state, tears me to shreds.

Adam was referring to the client who had arrived at the office to make his own funeral arrangements, leaving his young married daughter in the car outside. Although this was at least a decade ago, it was not unusual to plan the details of a funeral in advance, but the thought of paying for it at the time was rarely considered. This man was around forty years of age, pleasant, albeit a little nervous and smartly dressed. He had obviously given much thought to the arrangements for he knew exactly what he wanted. It was our custom in those days, to complete the form that we would normally use to note the details for a funeral at the time of need, and to simply omit the details relating to the death itself. This would enable us to make comprehensive arrangements, cover every aspect and as in this man's case, price the funeral. Part way through the interview, he was concerned about the gaps on the form in front of me, and wanted reassurance that my information was comprehensive. When I explained that the only gaps referred to the date, time and place of death, he responded by telling me that he had this information too. I sat there for some moments, wondering naively, what it must be like to know that you have a terminal illness and that the date of death was also predictable.

To Shed A Light

"I am sorry", I remarked. " I had no idea that you were ill".

"I am not", he replied. "I intend to take my own life and I can tell you exactly when that will be", he continued.

I put down my pen and spent an hour discussing the problems he had. His wife had died six months earlier and he had nothing to live for. His daughter had her own life to live and was fully aware of how he felt and what he intended to do. He had sought help from every source imaginable, but remained unconvinced. I tried desperately to find an answer, but I was running out of ideas and he was as calm and as determined as ever. I could not believe that anyone could plan so precisely, their own fate, yet alone talk through the details with a stranger. He knew what drugs to take, what the effect would be and how quickly they would act and therefore felt quite comfortable about the details on my form. After a lengthy discussion, the result of which I was not really sure about, I agreed to send him the cost of the funeral in the post, which was his main concern, and also planned to send him an amended quotation every year, to ensure that his savings could keep pace with the cost of funerals. In spite of this compromise, he insisted that the date of death would be 18th. September and would not go until I had recorded these details. We continued the rest of the interview as if it were a straightforward pre-planning exercise and did not refer to the circumstances again, but I remember watching his daughter driving away, and they both waved as they turned the corner. I felt relieved! Then I started to question the difference between client confidentiality and good sense. Should I be telephoning the various voluntary organisations that specialise in counselling the suicidal? He had already done that himself and got nowhere. Should I telephone the police? What could I tell them if I did? And why the 18th. September? It was early January, and the frost was on the ground and September seemed a million miles away and I was confident that our chat had helped somehow. As the months went by, I gradually forgot the experience, although whenever someone mentioned the word suicide, he sprang to mind and I would immediately check the date. The sun was shining brightly at the start of a good day, a day where everyone seemed ᵗ out of bed on the right side, when at lunchtiᵣ

To Shed A Light

approached by a young lady who had come to arrange her father's funeral. It was September 18th!

Adam was able to talk to Bob about other aspects which he would normally not discuss with a client, but their rapport was such that they felt comfortable in each others company and it gave Bob the confidence to discuss bereavement issues generally. This highlighted the genuine concern that Adam and all his staff seem to have when dealing with all aspects of the business which prompted Bob to ask about children's' funerals, a topic which Adam invariably covered when asked to give a talk on his profession, it being a topic that everyone seemed interested in. He started by explaining to Bob about the affect that the environmental health regulations have had on the funeral trade generally, and then elaborated about the babies in particular. Henshaw's, having a contractual arrangement with the hospital for dealing with all the 'non-viable' foetus', meant that they were conversant with all that was happening these days and Adam was pleased to tell Bob about the improvements that have been made in recent years in this respect. They became involved when the Environmental Health department condemned the hospital incinerator, and from then on, they were taken by the funeral director to the crematorium for cremation. Bob was impressed with the sensitive way in which Adam had dealt with this subject and the fact that throughout their chat, there was always a genuine emphasis on the care for the parents who are bereaved. For too long in the past, the loss of a baby had been treated like a non- event and Bob realised that both Adam and I, had influenced some of the changes that have taken place although that was not voiced. Bob had noticed the special crib arrangement in the chapel of rest, and it had been this that had encouraged him to broach the subject. The pastel shades that had been used to transform the drapes in the chapel so that they were more appropriate for a baby's funeral, added a touch that was impressive. The fact that this was recognised as being appropriate by the staff, rather than as a result of a request by the parents, confirmed in Bob's mind the genuine approach by all of Henshaw's staff, who were as enthusiastic about the desire to do that bit extra, as Adam and the rest of the management team were. It was at this point that Bob asked the question that was eating him away.

"I can understand now why you do the job, but I do not know how can you do babies funerals", he said.

"That's because you are focussing too much on the person who has died, rather than the people who are left", Adam replied.

"It is true to say, that if we were to sit and think long and hard about the circumstances and the tiny baby in particular, we would be unable to do the job, but look at it like this. Regardless of how old someone might be when they die, it is the effect that the death is having on the people that are left that we address. Some people, having lost elderly relatives are absolutely inconsolable. Others seem to take the death in their stride. Similarly, with the death of a youngster, the parents are often distraught, but also are often able to manage far better than you would think and this enables us to do our job. We just have to do whatever is necessary to arrange the details of the funeral to their complete satisfaction, and we have achieved what they want us to do. We can only do that if to some extent, we focus on the needs of those who are left, rather than the bereaved", Adam added.

Bob seemed satisfied with that explanation, for he felt that he had perhaps been inclined to dwell on the morbidity of the subject, rather than the practical angle.

There were other 'special circumstances' that happened on a regular basis, like the provision of a horse-drawn hearse, brass bands or pipers, all of which were unheard of as far as Bob was concerned. In an attempt to carry out the wishes of the bereaved it was often necessary to arrange for something unusual, or special as far as the bereaved were concerned, so Bob's requests were quite boring in comparison, and he now realised that Denise was right to change the arrangements and the funeral director. As good as Frank had been, his overall expertise did not compare with Adam's and at the end of the day the rest of the staff at the two different companies were certainly influenced by their individual leadership. Frank had touched briefly on the subject of Aids cases but was only describing some of the problems he has had in the past as a funeral director. Bob asked Adam if he had had a similar experience and was surprised when Adam smiled.

"The reason I am smiling", Adam immediately explained without further prompting, "Is because of the experience we had here at Henshaws' about a decade ago. It was about that time when 'Aids' cases suddenly became a problem. I do not know whether or not they had always been a problem and had only just been identified, or whether it was something quite new, but it caused a terrific scare for about three years. We first realised that something was wrong when the hospital porters would not transfer patients from the wards to the mortuary and then it was extended to the local community and they would not receive 'Aids' patients that had died at home, into the hospital mortuary where a Coroner's post-mortem was required. Many funeral directors and their staff also refused or were reluctant to handle the body and the Medical officer of health at the time was unable or unwilling to give any strong advice to funeral directors as far as the handling of the deceased was concerned. The hospital mortician at the time was satisfied that if sensible precautions were followed, there should be no danger, and when he was chatting to Peter on one occasion, found that he felt the same. As a result of this conversation, they both agreed to handle the patients on behalf of the district, moving them from the hospital ward to Henshaws' premises and then to be subsequently released to the funeral director who was to carry out the funeral, and if someone died at home, they would go to the house together and remove the deceased. This happened for about two years and during this time, they were on permanent call for this alone. Peter used to tell me how embarrassing it was, to turn up at someone's house, get togged up with all the recommended paraphernalia of boots, gown, mask, and gloves, to carry someone from the house to the hearse outside, watched by the family who had been nursing the patient for some time, wearing normal clothes. The fact that they understood and appreciated the fact that they were there at all did nothing to reduce the awkwardness they felt. Eventually, people started talking about HIV and the word 'Aids' was not used so much. It was appreciated that in terms of handling the patient, it was no worse than Hepatitis B and gradually the hospital porters took over the role at the hospital and other funeral directors began to handle the patients too. At the time of Peter's death, we would not even get to know that HIV was the possible cause of death and they are now handled with the same sensible precautions that should be adopted for any patient."

"What about the stigma attached to those deaths?" asked Bob.

"The stigma was and to some extent still is, the worst aspect about an 'Aids' related death", Adam continued. "Peter always used to say how pleased he was that the one thing he did not have to be, was judgmental about any aspect of his job and I have certainly taken that on board. He once told me about a client who had her son buried in a town many miles away from where she lived, so that the grave would remain intact. She always believed it would be vandalised because of the circumstances surrounding his death. She used to tell his friends and even some relatives that he had Cancer, because she could not bear the thought of him being without visitors. The other sad aspect, is that quite often, where the deceased's partner was of the same sex, they would rarely be invited to arrange the funeral or even share in the grieving process, and they would be left without comfort or recognition. The situation is better than it used to be now, but I often reflect on some of the cases that Peter experienced in those few years, knowing that there was so much ignorance and fear about the subject."

"Do you get excited when you have to deal with murders?" Bob asked, pushing his luck slightly.

"No, twenty years or so ago it might have been different, but they are almost commonplace now. At one time it would have been headline news, and now it scarcely makes the front page. Besides, dealing with the families of the victims is by no means exciting. When I think of all the bitterness, the guilt, the hatred, the disbelief and the mystery surrounding these deaths, I wonder they ever get organised. There are post-mortems for the Coroner, post-mortems for the defence and the publicity afforded to the funeral does nothing to help the bereaved family cope with their distress. The public find it interesting, and I suppose it sells newspapers and makes radio and television more attractive, but when you see the families sitting in your office to make the funeral arrangements, it puts things into a very different perspective. Peter always used to get annoyed when the newspapers refused his request to publish further details about an elderly person who had perhaps not achieved anything earth shattering, but who were just as important in the eyes of the bereaved, when in the next breath they would ask for further details about a youngster's death because they had read it in their own obituary column." Adam concluded.

"Surely someone who is really important is bound to get more publicity or when the circumstances are more tragic?" pursued Bob. "What about Princess Diana for instance?"

"It would take far more time than we can spend here today, to analyse Princess Diana's death and the repercussions, but let's quickly compare her death to Peter's. They both died in avoidable circumstances and their deaths are equally as tragic to the families concerned. Whenever Peter's colleagues said, "We must make a good job of this funeral because of the circumstances", Peter would always argue that everyone was important to someone and therefore deserving of the same 'special' treatment, and yet he too had the same soft spot for Princess Diana that most of the world seemed to share. He and Denise were on holiday in Ireland when her accident happened and like millions of others, they watched the funeral on a specially erected television screen in an hotel. Also like many others, Peter was reminded of his own mother's death and some of his tears at that time were for her too. It seemed to give the whole nation an opportunity to share in something that was common to them all and she will live on in their memories just as our own relatives live on in us. If our lives can be enriched by the influence that Diana has had, then perhaps her death will not have been in vain, but the tragedy of her sudden, unexpected and unexplained death will be remembered forever, whereas Peter's will fade more quickly." Adam glanced at his watch, almost unnoticed, but Bob took the hint. The only two items that Bob had not confirmed, were the cost of the funeral and the decision about paying in advance. The first one was easily dealt with, and although Henshaw's was probably around one hundred pounds more expensive than Dewbury & Fische Ltd. it was not so great that Bob felt obliged to change his mind, for he was now convinced that the overall service would be vastly superior. He smiled to himself as he realised that he would not be alive to verify that, but he had a shrewd idea that there would be little difference between the quality of his funeral, and mine.

As far as the peripheral services are concerned, Bob analysed the floristry and memorial side of Henshaw's business and was completely satisfied that, as they employ professionals in the field, there was no need to look elsewhere for these services. The printing of the hymn sheets had been organised by Adam, but through a local printing company. As the clergy seem to liase with the funeral director regarding the details of the service and also with the family for the selection of the hymns and music, there seems no good reason to take over the production of these, although in Bob's case, he probably would not require any, as his ceremony, lacking in religious content, would take place at the crematorium chapel. The catering after the funeral could easily be handled by Henshaw's staff, either at the house or on their own premises, and Bob decided to leave that decision to the people who would be responsible for making the final arrangements, when his death occurred.

Whilst Adam had not exactly talked Bob out of paying in advance for the funeral arrangements, he was certainly no more enthusiastic about it than I had been. Neither was there any need to make a decision immediately, but Bob was determined to think in terms of finding a plan to suit the funeral, rather than the other way round, if indeed he was to pursue this line of action. The one decision that Bob found difficult, was deciding on burial or cremation and he regretted at that stage having no-one around to help him to make that choice. Having a partner would have made the decision easier, but in the event, he had opted for burial in a cemetery where a traditional memorial would be allowed. He then took a leaf out of my book and asked Adam to purchase the grave space on his behalf, to ensure at least that there would be space available when the time comes. Quite apart from his reluctance to pay in advance for the funeral, Bob was also curious about what would happen if his relatives had no funds

To Shed A Light

immediately available to pay for the services he was arranging now. He was surprised to find that Henshaw's required no deposit and rarely needed any cast iron guarantee that the bereaved were able to pay. Adam's judgement over the years had been excellent, and he had rarely been let down. He did not wish to change the policy that had served the company well during my reign, and that comforted Bob. There were also other options available that had not been available elsewhere. They were licensed for credit and therefore could arrange for the family to pay monthly by standing order and were sympathetic towards any suggestion that would help their clients to pay more easily. There was no pressure to pay the account before probate had been granted, which was welcomed as far as the solicitors were concerned. However, if someone deliberately avoided payment, they would also take whatever steps were necessary to recover the debt.

There was only one pre-payment plan available that covered the costs of the funeral and the disbursements that would be paid out on behalf of the family. All the others offered by Henshaw's either included a contribution towards the disbursements, or paid only the funeral director's costs. Bob saw no point in a plan that only met part of the costs, and therefore decided to accept the plan which would ensure that the total cost of the funeral was covered. The arrangements that Adam had discussed with Bob were so comprehensive, that it was unlikely that any of Bob's relatives would need to enhance the package at the time of need. He came away from Henshaw's with a copy of the arrangements that he had organised, a pre-payment plan to cover the costs and adequate reading material regarding the services on offer and the after-care available for the relatives who would be left. One day, when the time was right, he would tell Denise what he had achieved, but felt at the moment that it would just add salt to her wounds.

Chapter Twelve

Denise invited Bob for a meal at a local restaurant to thank him for all he had done for her over the period, and especially for helping her to sort out the memorial. He accepted her invitation, although his eagerness to help had been by way of compensation for all that had gone wrong, in his eyes. He seized the opportunity to talk to Denise about some of his unanswered questions. He and I had spoken at length on many occasions about the way forward for funeral directing, but there had been no urgency to bring our discussions to any conclusion. Bob knew that Denise and I had chatted in greater depth about my vision, and because of all that had happened, he was now anxious to share those ideas.

"It seems like months ago now," he began. "Peter and I discussed in depth what he regarded as the best concept for the future, and although I realise that it is not so long ago, we never finished the conversation and I was fascinated by Peter's vision of how things could be. I also realise that if Peter could have afforded it, he would have put his ideas to the test, but they turned out to be dreams for him. I hope they will be a reality for someone else, but would you tell me in greater depth what his plans were?"

Denise smiled, for she knew that my ideas would never have come to fruition, even though she shared my enthusiasm. She knew also that I would never have had the money, and doubted whether or not I would have wanted to be the first to 'put my head above the trenches' if someone else had financed it, but she agreed to discuss it with Bob. She felt in the circumstances that this was the least that she could do.

"Before I tell you that," she replied, " I would just like to tell you that someone called David Soames did offer to back Peter's ideas once, but Peter thought that David's motives were not ethical and turned his offer down. I have often wondered how things would have turned out if he had taken the gamble. That is the problem when you try to analyse what might have been."

To Shed A Light

"Peter hinted that something like that had happened in the past, but he never elaborated. If the other person's sole aim in life was to make a fortune out of the project, I am not surprised that his offer was rejected," replied Bob.

"I do not think that Peter liked him very much either, and the fact that he was only financing the project rather than sharing his vision, did not help," Denise continued. They decided to skip the starter and just selected a main course and sweet from the menu, chatting comfortably over the meal.

"First of all, Peter insisted that it had to be the whole project, or nothing at all. There was never any question as far as he was concerned, of taking part of his idea and then gradually adding on the other aspects until his dream became a reality, but if I explain to you the whole concept, you will understand why this was so important to him."

"Do you mind if I make some notes while you are talking?" interrupted Bob.

"Not if you really want to, but don't let your meal get cold," Denise said, carrying on as if there had been no interruption.

"Peter's idea was based on the one objective of giving everyone a real choice about everything relating to bereavement, and this meant from the time of death right through to bereavement counselling, but it was incredibly complex. It started with the creation of a memorial park, on a site that would be close to all bus routes and with ample and easy access for off the road parking. The central point would be a new type of funeral home that would comprise the usual reception area, arrangement rooms, mortuary with embalming facilities, chapels of rest, and the essential office accommodation, but they would be designed as homely as possible, including bright decoration, soft furnishings and beautiful paintings on the walls, to make people feel comfortable at all times, whilst on the premises. The lighting would not be the harsh fluorescent lighting often associated with an office environment, but table and standard lamps and good quality carpet throughout. There would be no desks where the funeral arrangements were discussed in an attempt to make people feel more at home. There would be a crèche where trained staff would look after any children whilst their parents were organising the funeral details.

When the death occurs at home, the close family would be given the opportunity to accompany the deceased to the funeral home in an adapted 'people carrier'. This would have space for two or three family members and a special area to accommodate a coffin or stretcher where the deceased would lie. Once the embalming had taken place, a special family room would be made available where the relatives could, if they wished, help to wash, dress or generally prepare the deceased for the coffin. Accommodation would also be available for those relatives who needed it, until the day of the funeral. This is designed to give relatives the opportunity to say "goodbye" in their own time, without feeling pressured to observe some of the more traditional customs. They would be free to visit the chapel of rest at any time during their stay, and help to look after the person who has died, if they preferred to do so. There would be no secrecy about anything that happened on the premises, for the planning of the funeral, the treatment of the deceased and the care for the family would be of paramount importance, and the funeral itself would form only a small part of the overall support for the relatives.

There would always be an option to have a traditional funeral, with a church service and burial elsewhere with as much or as little involvement as the family wished. Alternatively, a service would be available where the deceased could be buried or cremated without anyone being present, and another brand new option, with an emphasis on the ceremony, rather than the 'disposal of the body', and therefore avoiding some of the 'traditional trappings' of a more familiar funeral."

Denise was aware that she had not spoken about this for some time, and gave Bob a sideways glance as if to ask if he wanted her to carry on, but she could see that he was intrigued.

"Carry on," he said as if she had asked the question.

"The emphasis would be on the new style of service, because this was what Peter thought was the best way forward," Denise continued.

"There was to be a small cremation facility within the grounds of the memorial park, but wherever possible the cremation process would be private. I'll tell you a bit more about the actual cremation part later. A family member could

To Shed A Light

witness this part, but it was hoped that this would be rare, for the emphasis was to be on the 'ceremony' in the building adjoining the chapel of rest.

This building, in many ways, would be like a traditional crematorium chapel, with a catafalque to support the coffin, an organ and other musical apparatus, and seating for one hundred and fifty people, but the emphasis would be on saying goodbye at the end of this part of the funeral, with the burial or cremation being done without anyone being present. Whether or not there would be any religious content for the ceremony, would be entirely up to the family to decide. There would be an opportunity to use the clergy employed at the memorial park, for part of the concept includes a bereavement advice centre where their expertise would be beneficial too, but there would also be trained personnel to lead the ceremony for those who prefer not to have any religious content. The arrangements where the family would normally use the minister from their own parish, would be the preferred option whenever a religious service was required, as this would also have the added benefit of a follow-up visit after the funeral. In trying to satisfy the needs of all the bereaved, a combination of both religious and secular expressions may often be appropriate in the one ceremony. An interdenominational Sunday service of remembrance would be held weekly, for all those who had died during the period, which would include input from people from all walks of life. They would all be united in their grief.

There would be a coffin showroom, similar to the one you saw at Henshaw's, but they would differ only in colour and design, rather than the price, because it would only be rented for the duration of the ceremony, and would consist only of an outer shell. The deceased would be placed in an inner disposable coffin, which would be taken out after the service had finished for the disposal of the body. In this way, the family could select something that was appropriate, whether it is an elaborate casket or a simple coffin, without worrying about any additional costs incurred. As the cremation would take place on the same site, there would be no need for a hearse or limousines. Relatives and friends would all make their way to the funeral premises and meet in an assembly room, adjoining a restaurant which would be used to provide meals for those relatives staying overnight on the premises, and also to provide refreshments for mourners when the funeral was over, and snacks for the daily visitors to the memorial garden. The assembly room would also be used to hold educational seminars, where outside speakers on specialist subjects relating to all aspects of bereavement, would be invited along to talk to an invited audience. Invitations would automatically be sent to all those using the facilities."

"Would there be an opportunity for anyone to pay their last respects before the funeral, if there is not to be a proper coffin?" asked Bob.

"Of course", said Denise. "Once the deceased has been dressed and laid in the inner coffin, this would be placed in the more elaborate coffin or casket selected, and then placed in the chapel of rest. The frill along the top edge of the hardwood coffin would hide the top edge of the disposable one and you would be able to pay your last respects in the normal way. In this respect, it would be no different, but the cost of an elaborate coffin would be eliminated. If the family preferred, they could see the deceased 'laid out' on a couch before being placed in the coffin."

"I am assuming that all these ideas about disposable coffins and hiring a hardwood casket are to reduce the overall cost of the funeral," said Bob.

"Partly cost, but more importantly, to address the environmental health problems that exist at the moment, and which will be much more strictly monitored and regulated in the future, if Peter's suspicions were accurate," responded Denise. "If you remember when Peter's funeral took place, I had him dressed in his own clothes," Denise continued. "Had he been cremated I would have had to think quite carefully about the clothes he was to wear because the man-made fibres of modern clothes have an adverse effect on the emissions from the crematorium flue. Peter thought they would be banned altogether in the future. As it is, there are restrictions about what items can be placed in the coffin and they are almost certain to become more strict about these aspects."

"Peter started to describe his ideas on burial too, can you remind me what they were," asked Bob.

To Shed A Light

"The Memorial Park would allow for a burial in the traditional manner, but the garden would be laid out in sections. There would be a place for woodland burial, but it would include a form of memorial too because Peter thought that was important. There would also be space for brick-lined graves. Traditional memorials with kerbstones would be encouraged, but instead of having grass between them, there would be gravelled paths for ease of maintenance. Lawn type sections would be provided for those who prefer only a headstone as a memorial but individuality in memorials of various sizes would be encouraged, rather than the regimental look often associated with military style cemeteries. The erecting of all memorials in the cemetery would be supervised by the cemetery superintendent to ensure that the fixing methods used conform to stringent fixing requirements to guarantee their long-term safety. There would also be space for well-planned areas for the interment of cremated remains, with or without a casket and with or without a memorial.

There would also be a number of children's play areas within the memorial park, to encourage normal activities that would not be disrespectful to those who had died, together with an area for the elderly and disabled to enjoy the tranquillity of a landscaped water garden. The wooded areas would be lit at night to encourage safe areas for the visiting bereaved at all times, and marked circular walks for those who wish to amble around the different areas of the park, unhindered."

At this point, Denise looked at the time, and realised that they had been talking for quite a while. Bob also realised that she was anxious about the time, and suggested that they finished their coffee and then carried on the discussion at home. The people at the next table were obviously uncomfortable with the topic of conversation because they looked relieved when Denise and Bob stood up to walk out of the restaurant. They said goodnight a little sheepishly and left, hoping their evening had not been spoilt. Denise was reminded of the occasion when she and I went out for a meal with her cousin and her husband, who is a veterinary surgeon, and we had discussed embalming and animal operations all evening, much to the disgust of the people at the tables within earshot. We had often laughed about that when we realised that they could hear every word.

In fact, once outside the restaurant, Denise and Bob decided that they should continue their discussion the next day, as it was so late, so Bob suggested that Denise went round for a drink at his house for a change. The next day, she called round as planned at eight o' clock in the evening, and for the first time since my death, almost felt guilty about being in Bob's company. Whilst she had felt alright in the restaurant, it seemed different somehow, alone in his house, but she overcame her discomfort after a short while and when she started to return to the subject in hand, completely forgot any misgivings she might have had.

"Where did we get to Bob?" she asked.

"You were describing the burial areas of the memorial park, according to my notes." Bob replied.

"Yes, Peter had strong views about the need to provide adequate opportunities to erect a memorial, but he also felt that there should be a change in the law regarding the re-use of burial plots. He thought that granting someone the exclusive right of burial in a grave for one hundred years, and then, after this period has expired, still being unable to re-use the grave for further interments without Home Office approval and often a Bishop's faculty too, has led to the unsafe condition of memorials and the unkempt state of burial grounds. He hated to see fallen and broken memorials in burial grounds, knowing that there were no relatives left to tend the graves, and was frustrated by the lack of will to do anything about it. Some countries have 'perpetually renewable licences' for graves, which means that there is an initial period of say fifty years granted to the 'owner' of the grave, on condition that the grave is kept in a tidy condition. The licence can be renewed after that time has elapsed, but this time for a much shorter period, possibly only five years at a time, the ongoing fees charged being used to carry out essential maintenance work at the cemetery. The option to renew the licence would be granted as often as necessary, but eventually, when there are no relatives left to continue the responsibility, the licence would not be renewed and the grave then re-used. Peter wanted this new memorial park to incorporate a similar idea, but he knew that at some point this matter would have to be discussed and dealt with sensitively. Any memorial on the grave would be disposed of, and a new permanent remembrance plaque would be erected on the perimeter wall. When the grave is prepared for subsequent burials, any remains found would be collected together and reburied in the base of the new grave. Peter had assumed that by the time this concept became a reality, the law would have changed to allow the 'disturbance' of human remains in those circumstances, without the need to apply for permission from the Home Office in each individual case. In the meantime, he suggested that family sized plots should be encouraged, so that there may be more members of a family who would be interested in the maintenance of the grave."

"It will be a brave person to bring this whole subject to the notice of those who are in a position to do something about it." Bob said.

"It is such a sensitive subject and a very personal one too. There is not always a logical argument for change, or for the 'status quo' for that matter, but the shortage of space will eventually force a decision. I just hope they allow the time for consultation before the need arises to do something," replied Denise.

"Surely the funeral directors will not like this concept that Peter was so keen on, because they will make less money," suggested Bob.

"The services provided would be different, giving the bereaved a better opportunity to select much more carefully, those elements which are important to them, some of which may not be available now and in this respect the opportunities could be far better for those funeral directors who are able to share in the wealth of facilities that the concept requires, although it would mean having to work differently. Nevertheless, there will be those who for one reason or another would not be able or willing to compete or join forces and would therefore be totally against the new ideas, but it is not only those funeral directors that would be displeased. This was part of the problem," continued Denise. "In fact, funeral directors would certainly lose some income, because the cost to the family would be greatly reduced, although the cost of providing the new service would also be less expensive. The other problem, is that the local crematorium and cemetery authorities would also lose business."

"The other integral part of Peter's plan, was to have as an extension of the funeral home, a florist's shop, a memorial workshop, a bereavement advice centre and a bereavement support club."

"How would these work?" asked Bob.

"The florists shop would be open only for funeral tributes, and cut flowers for the chapel decoration or for placing on graves and other designated areas within the park. The groundsmen would also obtain any bedding plants for the gardens from the in-house florist. The staff employed to run the shop would also be trained in bereavement counselling so that they could appreciate the stress encountered by those close relatives ordering funeral tributes.

One of the main functions of the advice centre, would be to provide a drop-in centre for all those wanting to contact Cruse, S.A.N.D.S., Compassionate Friends or other similar bereavement related organisations who could be represented on the site. Immediate counselling would be available for those who needed urgent assistance. A supply of literature describing all the facilities at the memorial park would be handed out and they would also refer people on to the bereavement support club. This would be run by a group of 'befrienders', whose aim in life would be to form a group of like-minded bereaved people who are either lonely or finding it difficult to cope. They would meet as a group to support each other in their grief and to offer practical solutions to the day to day problems that invariably crop up. The bereavement support club is meant to achieve far more than provide an ear and a cup of coffee. Day classes would be held to teach new skills to those who have relied on their partner for help in the day to day running of the home. Cooking, cleaning, washing, ironing, shopping, and round the house practical help like mending a fuse and changing a light bulb would all be taught to those who needed help in order to create a new feeling of confidence and independence. Volunteers from this support group would also help to make the 'hotel' guests more comfortable, by practising the skills they are taught in the day classes. There would be no charge for the day classes and no payment for their hotel duties. Recognising that people need a reason to get out of bed in the morning and something to look forward to, produced the germ of this idea. Mixing with others who would understand something of how they feel and an opportunity to practice some of the new skills learned at the various workshops would, hopefully, give them a purpose in life, initially at least.

The memorial workshop would be unique. Part of it would be devoted to selling and producing memorials for the graves in the Memorial Park and for graves at other local cemeteries and churchyards, but there would also be practical demonstrations of hand carving in stone and hands-on training for those who wish to help produce a finished memorial. There would be educational days to learn about the different types of materials used to manufacture memorials and machine cutting and sandblasting techniques. Garden furniture, house nameplates and other types of memorial possibilities would also be demonstrated.

They would also discuss those areas of memorialisation which are not available on the site but that could be considered as additional or alternative suggestions"

"You were going to mention something else about the cremation," Bob reminded Denise.

"One of the difficulties that would need to be overcome," Denise answered, "is the need to differentiate between the authority allowing the cremation to take place and the funeral directors who would be responsible for the management of all other aspects in the park. In other words, having the two functions on the same site would necessitate having to enforce the strict code of cremation practice that exists already, to enable the cremation to be authorised and supervised by an independent medical referee who would not be employed by the owners of the memorial park. It would be important to ensure that these two roles, for legal reasons, were kept separate, but in reality, despite the fact that the idea would be frowned upon initially, it is perfectly possible to operate the crematorium as a separate unit, in exactly the same way as all other privately owned and managed crematoria, but on a shared site. I suppose there was opposition to the invention of the wheel, but we seem to have overcome those problems," she added.

"I know this is nothing to do with what you are talking about now," Bob interrupted, "but Peter also told me about the cremated remains and insisted that I never called them ashes. He was also talking about his library in the same breath, and I have to confess that he lost me there. Do you know what he was talking about?"

"It is simple, really," Denise explained. " Ashes are what you get as a result of burning something! As far as the cremation is concerned, the bones do not burn, and so they are taken out of the cremator after the process has finished and pulverised in a machine and recovered afterwards for disposal. They are what remain after the cremation process has been completed, and so they are called 'cremated remains'. As the bodies are cremated separately, there would be no doubt about the family receiving the correct remains for interment or scattering afterwards. However, the majority of people today, do refer to them as 'ashes', which makes it even more difficult for funeral directors to refer to them by their proper name. There is another problem though, that causes as much distress as anything else, and that is the need to make a decision about what is to happen to them, before the near relatives are ready to do so. Peter's idea at the memorial park, to overcome the need to insist on an early decision, was to create a library to store the cremated remains until a decision could be made, similar to the one he created at Henshaw's. The 'books' would be made of wood and be identified with a number on the spine and the written details enclosed. A book of remembrance would be introduced, to serve two purposes. It would be used to locate the remains in the library and would also be available for mourners to read on the anniversary of the date of death. At the base of each shelf unit, would be a trough containing plants and flowers, with an opportunity for mourners to leave their own cut flowers in the containers provided. In this way, there would be no urgency for a decision to be made, less risk of the family having any regrets and an opportunity to visit the 'library chapel' as often as they wished."

To Shed A Light

"I know that you said it was complex," said Bob. "But I had no idea it was as involved as this. It is no wonder Peter wanted to create the concept in its entirety from day one."

"The grieving process is a complicated one, and made worse by the fact that it follows no set pattern. No two individuals are going to grieve in the same manner and that is why Peter wanted all the help available on one site. He also felt that if the support was generally available, no-one would feel embarrassed about using it. Their needs are different but often they are helped by seeing others struggling too, for so intense are the emotions sometimes, that they want confirmation that they are not going mad and that others too, feel just as hurt in their sorrow. Starting off with a site that would provide only some of these facilities, would be like setting up a service that could only address some of the problems" explained Denise.

"Was Peter expecting to finance the whole project himself?" Bob asked.

"Peter was never expecting to get it off the ground. It was an ambition that was never likely to be achieved, even though his death was premature. However, the concept is a good one and has better prospects for the future than it might have done in the past," replied Denise.

"I thought Peter wanted others to be involved with the concept, as opposed to going it alone," suggested Bob.

"He did! It is not the sort of project for a one-man band. His idea was to set up a group of like-minded experts who would concentrate on their own areas of expertise. The funeral directors would do what they do best, as would the florists, the memorial masons, the crematorium and cemetery authority, the caterers, the medical team, the financial advisers, the bereavement organisations and so on," Denise agreed.

"I must have been asleep when you mentioned the medical team and the financial advisers," interrupted Bob.

"There were a few other aspects to the project that we have not mentioned yet," said Denise.

"There would be a solicitor and a financial adviser on the site to advise on legal and financial matters and a representative of the Citizens Advice Bureau to help with any claims for financial assistance through the Social Security or any other family problems but they would also help with the educational sessions when it came to giving advice about how to write a cheque for the first time, or open a bank account or simple instructions on the best way to pay various bills. There could be a rota to man these offices so that the benefits were shared between members of the different professions," she added.

"Let us have a drink," suggested Bob.

"Wait a few minutes, Bob. I have nearly finished and then you can do what you like," Denise said, smiling. She carried on without waiting for a response.

"One of the problems at many cemeteries is the maintenance of the grounds and the potential problems associated with vandalism. Peter thought that if the schools were involved with the project, there would be less vandalism and a better kept memorial park. His idea was to have ongoing competitions in local schools for the construction of new areas within the park, for the burial of cremated remains, with new ideas about memorialisation. The park would adopt the best schemes and the school would help to maintain the area they had designed, in return for a donation to school funds. This in turn would encourage the children to see the memorial park as an amenity for the local community, and would help with their nature studies with the planting of wild flowers in the woodland and other areas of the park. The only other area that we have not mentioned is the medical centre, which would be there to provide medical support to all who visit the site and provide district nursing for those bereaved persons who need support at home. If Peter had any other ideas about the park, he kept them to himself or I have forgotten them," said Denise.

Denise had shown an artist's impression of the memorial park to Bob, and seeing it on paper almost made it a reality but it was far from ever being viable as a project during my lifetime. There were too many hurdles to leap, too much commercial opposition, and it was too expensive for any individual to contemplate. The whole idea was a threat to traditional funeral directing methods and the industry has always been reluctant to adopt new ideas, especially radical ones of this nature. Everyone is entitled to have an unfulfilled dream or two and as naïve as my optimism might have been, this was to be mine. If a few professionals with a similar vision for the future were to get their heads together and form a consortium to share the costs and management of the project, it could still become a reality, and the benefits to the bereaved would be tremendous, but the contentious issues involved may be too emotive to handle for all but the tenacious, in an industry which is not yet ready for such a dynamic change of direction.

As interested as Denise and Bob were in the whole idea, Bob was too old and Denise too tired to contemplate any involvement in anything so challenging, but talking about the way forward had helped Denise to 'put to bed' some of the baggage she has been carrying since my death. Whilst in the process of discarding my personal items, no longer required and taking up space, she had come across the sketches and the written details that I had compiled about the project, and had read them properly for the first time, so she was quite pleased to have the opportunity to share the whole idea with Bob, knowing that I had confided in very few people about the scheme since I first put pen to paper, but aware that Bob was one of them. At least now she could file the paperwork away, although she was still reluctant to part with it altogether. This was true of much of what she had sifted through. Some of it made her smile, some of it made her angry or upset, but in her attempt to discover whether or not something was worth keeping, she felt as if she was invading my privacy and it took her a long while to complete the task. These documents were the last to be dealt with and she felt better now.

"Now we can have that drink you threatened me with earlier," said Denise, relieved that she no longer had to answer any more of his questions.

They chatted more comfortably now, about all manner of things, but agreed to leave me out of the conversation, having talked, it seemed, about nothing else for so long. Bob poured a couple of drinks and they were soon discussing their holiday plans. Bob's favourite haunt in this country was Tenby, which immediately brought back happy memories for Denise. Some

To Shed A Light

of our happiest days had been spent in Pembrokeshire when Luke and Jane were small and she smiled as she tried to relate to those times without mentioning my name. She remembered the days when Luke and I had been rock pooling on the beach in Tenby while she and Jane had been sunbathing nearby.

To reminisce about the Scilly Isles, which has been heaven on earth for us both, for many years, without uttering my name was not only difficult, but unnecessary too. They both realised that if my name cropped up naturally in conversation, it would be acceptable, and as Denise had already made plans to go to there for her next holiday, they would either have to change the subject, or allow her the odd reference here and there, knowing that we had spent so much time together at the Scillies, over the last fifteen years. I had been wondering whether or not Denise would be able to pluck up the courage to go again, because so much of our time had been spent there, and it had always been the most relaxing of holidays. But above of all, it was by the sea and Denise was as happy as I have ever seen her when she was at the seaside. Our timeshare on Tresco had enabled us to enjoy the islands on an annual basis, but this time she was going to St. Marys, the largest of the islands, with an ulterior motive.

Since my death, I have been conscious of the fact that whenever Denise has been distraught, I have been able to see her more clearly. When she has been happy, my clouds have been grey and opaque and my sight dimmed. At first, when she was experiencing more bad days than good, I could see her almost all of the time, such were her endless days of grief, but as the months have passed by, the anniversaries overcome and the memories begin to fade, Denise is now experiencing more good days than bad. It feels odd knowing that she is happy and that I cannot share in her pleasure, yet I have to witness her pain. Perhaps she can sense my yearning when she is at her most vulnerable and gain comfort from that experience because she does not need me on a good day for her own strength is sufficient. I feel like a chrysalis waiting to be hatched, with the occasional glimpse of the life I have left, but no knowledge of what is to come. My zone is timeless, and without light or heat, for I no longer need those comforts for my survival, but on the rare, sad days now, when I can see Denise, my cocoon splits open momentarily and I rely on the

To Shed A Light

warmth of the sun to generate my support for her. They are usually specific memories of our happiest times together that produce Denise's dullest moments for it is at these times that she wants me back again, and she is aware that this cannot be, but the frequency of these desperate moments is becoming less and less. One day she will be able to share her life with someone else, without the feelings of guilt that still torment her.

We had talked about our future without each other and the way we might feel about new relationships, and I had always been comforted by the fact that she would feel able to love someone else, without detracting from the life we had shared. Bob's friendship was genuine and any doubts I might have had about that initially were dispelled long ago. Nevertheless, he is still a true friend. They are not really suited and despite her vulnerability of recent months and his eagerness to comfort her, Denise had resisted the temptation to cry on his shoulder and risk a liaison that neither of them wanted.

Her journey to the Scilly Isles has been planned for some time. Denise still has her own dreams to realise and retiring to the Islands whilst she is still active and healthy, has become her main ambition. She can afford to buy a small cottage on St. Mary's and spend the rest of her days in her own peaceful haven. Luke and Jane and other close family members will no doubt holiday there with their partners in the future, and Denise will come back to the mainland occasionally to see her relatives and friends. She will have time to reflect on our life together and I shall be able to measure the extent of her happiness by the darkness of the clouds.

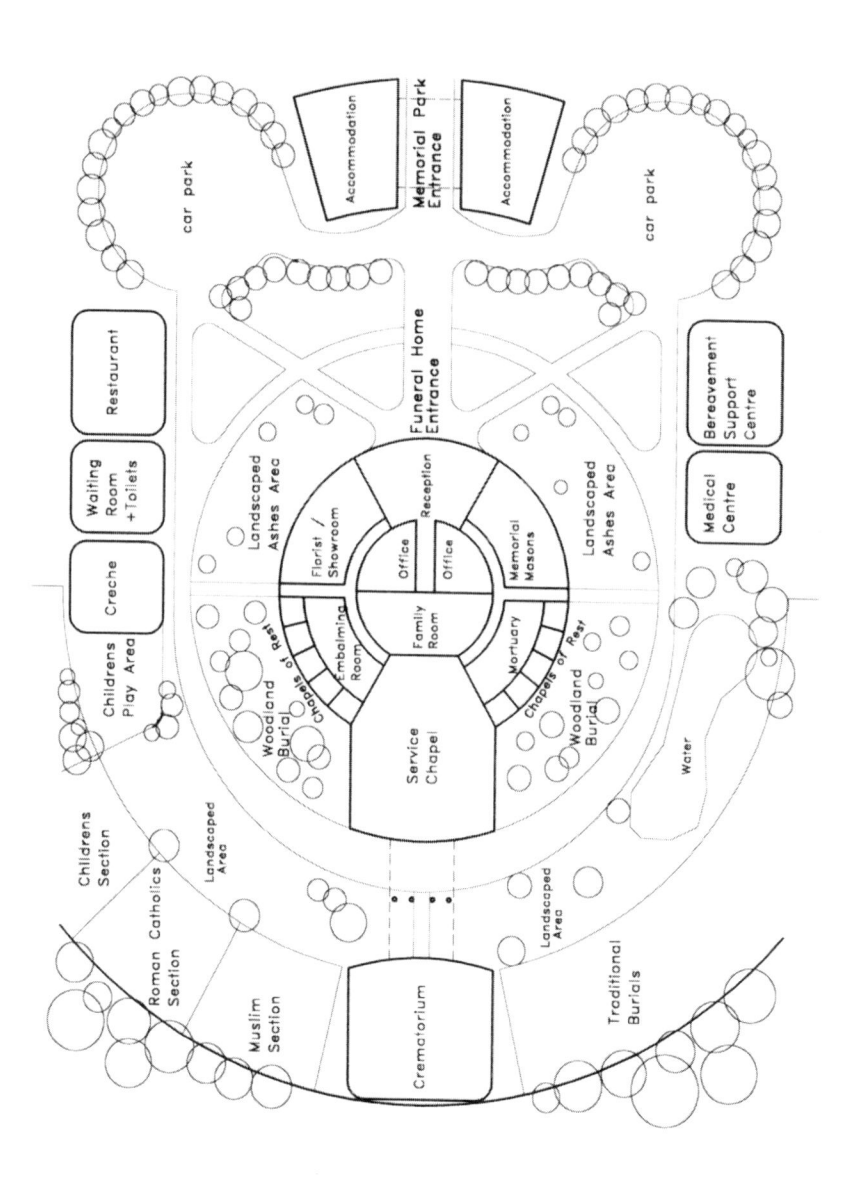

An artist's impression of Peter's vision for the future.